GW00361499

Other Books by This Author

The Promise
The King's Sword
The Bone Cartouche

KING HAROLD II

The Norman Conquest and what he did next.

AN ENGLISH STUDY OF THE TRUE LIFE AND NATURE OF KING HAROLD II

PETER BURKE

authorHOUSE®

AuthorHouse™ UK
1663 Liberty Drive
Bloomington, IN 47403 USA
www.authorhouse.co.uk
Phone: UK TFN: 0800 0148641 (Toll Free inside the UK)
UK Local: 02036 956322 (+44 20 3695 6322 from outside the UK)

© 2021 Peter Burke. All rights reserved.

No part of this book may be reproduced, stored in a retrieval system, or transmitted by any means without the written permission of the author.

Published by AuthorHouse 02/24/2021

ISBN: 978-1-6655-8634-4 (sc)
ISBN: 978-1-6655-8633-7 (hc)
ISBN: 978-1-6655-8635-1 (e)

Print information available on the last page.

Any people depicted in stock imagery provided by Getty Images are models, and such images are being used for illustrative purposes only. Certain stock imagery © Getty Images.

This book is printed on acid-free paper.

Because of the dynamic nature of the Internet, any web addresses or links contained in this book may have changed since publication and may no longer be valid. The views expressed in this work are solely those of the author and do not necessarily reflect the views of the publisher, and the publisher hereby disclaims any responsibility for them.

FOREWORD

It is known there is an ancient book, kept secret for four hundred years, read only by the monks of Waltham to remind them of the true story and the goodly nature of their former king and patron, Harold Godwinson, the last Saxon king of England

～

This is the English version of the myth the Chester Hermit, a curious and ancient tale discarded by Norman chroniclers and labelled as lies by historians from ancient times till now. This is the truth of those times, and it has been too long in the telling.

The Last Confession of William I

I've persecuted the natives of England beyond all reason, whether gentle or simple. I have cruelly oppressed them and unjustly disinherited them, killed innumerable multitudes by famine or the sword, and become the barbarous murderer of many thousands young and old of that fine race of people, having gained the throne of that kingdom by so many crimes, I dare not leave it to anyone but God to judge.
—Orderic Vitalis

CHAPTER 1

'We write of things we read of but have not seen, by the laws of histories told, the truth of the writer is assured, whereas the truth of those events be wrecked.'

This is a quote from the writer of events in the twelfth century. The writer was concerned that, though he knew what he was recording was true, he was aware that others who did not have his knowledge were writing off those same events he was recording, but with a bias towards the ruling class.

His concerns were justified. History as we read and accept it, in this particular case, has come down to us as they recorded, and the recordings of the historian who wrote the initial history—his account of events—has been forgotten. Time passes, an account is accepted, and the truth is wrecked.

It underlines the need for historians to write our histories accurately and honestly, recorded from their own findings and not based on personal thoughts or guesswork.

The problem we have is that too many who go through the system in education, and particularly that of historical studies, accept the versions of history passed on to us from those who go before. Many of these were pastors or closely associated with the church in some form or another. So those confirmed events in history come down to us as they happened, and we accept and acknowledge them, yet there is a lack of understanding as to the details and questions that need to be answered as to why some of these main events happened in the first place. The recording of history is not just a process of writing down events, because as a people who look forward in order to improve and gain understanding, we also need to see clearly that journey we have taken and how we got here.

1

This subject is an example. We have numerous mentions from historians going back into the past who look at documented assertions and dismiss them because they are seen as inconsistent as an acceptable piece of our history.

Although this new evidence we have found will not change our history—yes, William invaded England, and Harold was defeated—it will lift the lid on some of the injustices and slurs that pepper this period, giving a very different view of those back then who were the main characters in this, the most important time in English history.

Obviously, it is impossible to research all events in our history, and it follows that we will never know everything, so our history will never be complete. This means there will always be gaps to be filled. Yet these infills should be well chosen.

Any of us can write and rewrite, tweak and change the details, but like an art restorer who works on an original piece of artwork and understands the weight of responsibility he holds, he will ensure that his efforts do not endanger the authenticity of the original work so that the true representation is retained, for if this is not the case, then what we end up looking at is not authentic at all but is a lie.

It is not my intention to confuse the history in this piece but to reveal fresh evidence that directly contradicts established history about the most dramatic period of change England, and the English, experienced. I am no different than many who happen upon a fable and allow themselves to imagine for a moment that what they are reading could perhaps have an element of truthfulness within the story.

I am happy to admit that as I read for the first time about this seemingly preposterous tale—that King Harold, he with the arrow in his eye, could have survived that momentous battle at Hastings and go on to live a long, peaceful life as a travelling pilgrim—I allowed myself a moment of indulgence as my mind wandered into the what-if hypotheses.

How I came upon this tale was by chance. I was spending a great deal of time researching a period in history, the Bronze Age, in Crete because I planned to write a novel based around the Minoan civilisation. It was a story that came down through time to our day, and what I needed was a story that was plausible. It did not have to be fictitious, but if it was different? This was the kind of story I was looking for. Factual or fictitious, this story needed to grab me so I could weave it into the plot.

It also needed to be a kind of cameo from history that people would be familiar with in order to connect threads from our day in England right back through time to the Bronze Age in Crete.

It was while searching through reams of reference works that I came across the Fancy, as historians like to call it. The story is about a king who became a hermit. It was a perfect fit, a little-known tale dating back to the early twelfth century. A handful of historians have, over the years, given consideration to this curious tale and will agree it is a fable, akin to Aesop's, with a message. I concur that at the time, I believed it to be a fable, but I found it strangely beguiling.

I enjoyed writing the Promise trilogy. I loved the journey of being totally engrossed in the plot and finding the largely unknown history of the Minoan civilisation totally enthralling. I came upon an idea while I was on holiday with my first wife, Julie, in a small town known as Agios Nikolaos on the northern coast of Crete. It was around this time that an English worker from Liverpool had been executed by terrorists in the Middle East.

I wondered at how people can justify killing anyone by saying, 'God wills it.' I found it repugnant, and it reminded me of the barbarity of the Crusades.

I imagined a scenario where a seemingly 'normal' man from Barnet was kidnapped by terrorists, but while caught up in a blinding fanaticism, what they failed to see was that this chap was one of a protected line, a special one, protected by the very God these kidnappers claimed to work for.

When the story came to a finish, I found this strange tale of the hermit king would not let me rest. It was as if there was a little voice, somewhere at the back of my mind, asking me to look again.

I cannot always rein in the excitement I experience when discovering some fresh, new evidence. My most ardent desire is to write down these exciting moments and not keep them to myself.

I make no apologies for these occasional moments of exuberance, because this is a tale long overdue in the telling, and I am certain if you share my love of history, you will also share my enthusiasm.

A Question of Discernment

Is our recorded history correct in the detail? No. Is there a danger that as we add more researched matter to our established history, instead of tearing down the dusty drapes and decluttering the reams of hypotheses that block out the light in our effort to enhance our understanding of our past, we further obscure our history?

The details in our history, delivered to us by the schools and universities, are a covering of those important events in our history, but through history there are always those 'between the lines' events that are not so well documented and are mostly guesswork. We are given an overview of the major historical events that have shaped our world and our culture.

Here, then, we are presented with a dilemma. We have libraries full of historic records, reference works written over centuries by countless recorders of our history. We have countless versions of our histories in which those recorders added conjecture as to the reasons and motives that influenced those key players at the time. These records are used as research tools, in our quest to find the truth.

It has become an impossible task to assimilate all this learning and conclude for our own satisfaction what truth is! Is the best we can hope for, then, merely an approximate understanding of the past?

New Evidence

When new evidence comes to light, it is right that the discoverers of this evidence reveal this so that it can be examined as to its validity. It may also serve to inform those keepers of our histories so that the necessary adjustments to our records can be made.

In this publication, there is, for the first time in over nine hundred years, compelling evidence that tells us we need to change our history. I seriously doubt that this will happen, so I implore the reader to have patience and read on with an open mind. Join me on this extraordinary adventure, and experience that precious enlightenment that comes from discovering something new.

I have always taken issue with a dismissive attitude towards any evidence that comes to light, that disagrees with the established norm. In my mind, it is pure laziness if we discard evidence without carrying out a thorough search. That is simply sloppy.

In our education system, the histories are accepted and taught as set out in our textbooks.

I know that a good teacher will advise his students, if they are to be able to accept and move on with their learning, that they must look into their subject with a critical eye, and, after an exhaustive period of research and a balanced cross-section of available study material, make up their own minds as to the truth, but based on the material studied that's worthy.

Not that I ever listened to my former tutors, because most times my scheduled days of schooling were often spent in the woods at Hadley. Hadley was a minor province in the southern part of the county of Hertfordshire, England. This place and other locations close by are where one would find me wandering the quiet streets of New Barnet, wondering when it would be safe to return home, having spent my five bob dinner money at the corner cafe on the corner of St Margaret's Road.

I had no watch and so had to hang around at the end of our road until I saw the other kids from my school returning home. Watches were for posh kids, and school education was not recognised or appreciated as being the only path to true wealth and riches.

This attitude was quite normal on our street, and the same was true of many other kids my age. The path to wealth and riches was a job at Holdrups, a concrete products factory on Bells Hill.

However, I did manage to battle through my school years and emerge at the other end pretty well unscathed, having learned to dodge blackboard eraser and detention. Quite a feat for the son of a hod carrier from the poorer end of town.

Let's return to the subject of our much-maligned Saxon king, Harold Godwin. It's not easy when opinions are divided on a subject, and simply having access to a wide range of research material will not always resolve an issue. This is particularly true in the case of Harold's death. Most research material will tell you that at the Battle of Hastings, Harold died, period. Deciding what study material to go through is crucial to a student if the student is to form a judgement that is fair. This includes, most importantly, the new evidence we have found.

Let's look at the subject under scrutiny, King Harold II, the last Saxon king of England.

The myth of Harold tells us he survived the battle in 1066. History tells us he died with an arrow through his eye. The foremost questions are as follows.

> In 1066, did Harold Godwin die or survive?
> If he survived, what evidence is there?
> Is it really possible to find evidence that he survived the Battle of Hastings after 960 years?

Normally if you, the reader, are familiar with the events of 1066, then going over those events again would not be very informative. You would have heard it, read about it, been taught it at school, and so find it a little tedious going through it again. However, if I take you through the events of that year, armed with our clearer understanding of those times and events based on those new findings we have discovered, then the story will unfold differently.

It would be helpful first to look at some of those events that shaped the politics in England leading up to the battle, and the state of the country after.

Harold was the second son of Earl Godwin and was born around 1022. It is said that he was 'high' born, meaning he was educated in the Saxon manner, to be groomed for an eventual earlship.

However, we have discovered that he was certainly more than that. He was from the line of Aethelred, King Alfred's elder brother and former king of Wessex, but I will go through this later.

We know from the records at the time that he was an intelligent youth of good manners and was well liked. He was loyal to his older brother Sweyn and his younger brothers, but as events unfolded, his loyalty was to be tested.

In 1046, at the age of twenty-six, Sweyn sided with Gruffydd ap Llywelyn against Deheubarth in the south of Wales in a power struggle between the two claimants to the Welsh throne. His reasons for befriending Gruffydd were likely political, because the Earldom of Sweyn bordered the Welsh kingdom of Deheubarth in the south.

As Sweyn returned from battle, he seduced the Abbess of Leominster, and when he asked King Edward for permission to take her hand in marriage, he refused.

It was a slight against his position as earl, and looking over the events that followed, it is clear the balance of his mind was disturbed from this time because he continued on a path that could do no more than to end badly.

It is recorded that after two terms of banishment, a barefooted pilgrimage to Jerusalem in an attempt to redeem himself from the murder of his cousin, and open rebellion, a seemingly unrelated event was to end his life. He was murdered at Constantinople on his return from Palestine.

For us, without making assumptions and with so complex a set of circumstances, it would be hard to empathise with Sweyn. And yet remembering that, although these characters were giants of their time, they were still human, and subject to the normal feelings, and frailties born of a family of so complex a circumstance, being so concerned with power, identity, position, and pride.

Looking back over the life of Sweyn, we may well consider his circumstances and understand what turmoil he wrestled with considering those events that shaped him. While still a youth, Sweyn was secretly told that his actual father was not Earl Godwyn but the king at the time, Cnut. This fundamentally changed the dynamics in the family, so much so that Sweyn, convinced by these rumours, challenged his mother.

His mother, Gytha, denied this accusation and publicly announced it in an attempt to deflect unwanted, shameful attention from herself. This was the beginning of the discord that, from this time on, plagued the Godwyns.

Sweyn had become earl of lands that bordered the Welsh in the south while he was still quite young. He sought to find his place in the power struggle that had risen within the family, causing much uncertainty and unrest.

The old earl, Harold, sought the favour of Edward using the newly formed marriage of the king to his daughter, Edith. This marriage had been a rocky relationship from the beginning. Edward would not consummate the marriage and still had strong ties to Normandy, where he had previously spent many years.

Edward was a weak king in some areas. He felt the need to retain some loyalty to Normandy but accepted he had a duty to the English. An incident at Dover resulting in the visiting nobleman Eustace II of Boulogne being chased out of Dover embarrassed him.

As punishment for not cracking the whip at his men in Dover, Earl Godwyn and his family were exiled to Flanders, yet later in his reign, Edward came to seriously reflect on his own responsibility as king of the English.

At the time, the incident between local people loyal to the Godwyns and the Norman knights had left some Normans dead. Earl Godwyn had refused the king's request to deal harshly with his people, and this was why the Godwyn family were exiled. This was in 1051. In 1052, after both Harold and Leofwyn had fled to Dublin, armies were raised, and the two joined their father and returned to England with a sizeable army, forcing Edward to give back Earl Godwyn's lands and reinstate the family to power.

After the death of Sweyn in Constantinople and the death of the old earl at a banquet in Winchester, Harold inherited the Earldom. At this time, there was no indication of a conflict between Harold and his younger brother Tostig as they embarked on a campaign against Gruffedd ap Llywelyn, the former ally of Sweyn. In 1063, they forced the surrender of the Welsh.

Tostig returned to his earldom in the north, and Harold returned to Winchester to report to Edward the king. News of his quashing the rebellion of Gruffydd ap Llywelyn and the delivering of the old Welsh king's head made the rounds.

How these events unfolded, and how peace between Edward and the Welsh was accomplished, we believe started when a prince of Gwynedd, Cynan ap Iago, son of the former king of Gwynedd, returned from exile in Dublin and joined in the war against Harold and Tostig. On the lower hills of Snowdonia, in the summer of 1063, when the beleaguered force of Gruffydd ap Llywelyn sought safety from the Saxon army, Cynan ap Iago slew the stubborn old Welsh king and removed his head.

It was this act that finally brought some peace to the country, although this was not to be the end of the matter, and certainly this act of regicide was not undertaken with the same fabled willingness of King Bendigeidfran of the 'feast of the wonderous head'. Gruffydd ap Llywelyn was not coming back, even though some may have been in awe of the man and wished it so.

He had proved himself a mighty Welsh king who had taken his people in rebellion both to the east, across England, and to the west, to Ireland.

Bleddyn ap Cynfyn was made king and ruled well for twelve years but was not revered as his predecessor was. Neither was he afforded the same respect.

The Legend of the Feast of the Wonderous Head

I feel it will be helpful to say something about this Welsh and Irish legend because it conveys to us a little of the history of those people back then, the nature of their storytelling, and their beliefs. It also shows how a story can be so easily influenced by people's beliefs in the supernatural. I say this only as a way of us being able to distinguish and understand the difference between a myth and a recording of actual events.

The legend tells of a beautiful girl who was the sister of the king of the Britons. Her beauty became known to the king of Ireland, Matholwch. Her name was Branwen-Ferch-LLyr. She had two brothers, Bendigeidfran, who was the king, and Manawydan, a giant with mystical powers. These were watching the sea from Harlech Hill when they saw a great fleet of ships arrive and dock below the great hill at Harlech. As they watched, a shield was held aloft for them to see that the purpose of their visit was peaceful.

It was Matholwch, and he had come to ask for the hand of Branwen in marriage. The king and his family agreed that it was a good match that would bring about peace between the two countries. There was one though, who had not approved the match. This was the half-brother to Branwen-Ferch, Efnisien, who had been off hunting.

The wedding was held at the great hall in Aberffraw on Anglesey, and as all drank and celebrated heartily, Efnisien returned. He was outraged that he had not been informed, and he harboured great animosity against the king of Ireland. He took his sword and maimed the horses of the Irish entourage. A great argument broke out as the happy feast turned sour, however the king of the Britons, Bendigeidfran, calmed all and called for

9

an apology from Efnisien. This was reluctantly given, and the lost horses were replaced.

Bendigeidfran made an offering to Mtholwch of a magic cauldron that was said to be able to return the dead to life. This was very pleasing to the Irish king.

Branwen-Ferch returned to Ireland with her new husband, and all was well. She became pregnant and bore a son, Gwern, but when the disrespectful behaviour of Efnisien and the harm he has caused the horses of their king became widely known, they demanded that Branwen-Ferch be punished for her half-brother's actions.

She was sent to work in the kitchens and beaten regularly there. For three years she suffered, and her family had no knowledge of this, believing she was well and flourishing. While working in the kitchens, she befriended a starling, a small speckled bird, and she slowly taught it to recognise her brother.

Then one day, she tied a message to its wings and sent it off to Wales, to find her brother. The bird flew across the sea and landed in Caernarfon. It was found by a youth and taken to the king, and the king called together his army.

The fleet set sail, and Bendigeidfran himself waded across the sea. Before the two armies engaged in war, a message was sent to Bendigeidfran from the Irish king, Matholwch.

The Irish king promised he would give the kingdom to his son, Gwern, who was the nephew of Bendigeidfran. It was a solution that was to bring about peace between the two countries, and it would have worked had not Efnisien seen this as a trick.

As the boy came before his uncles to greet them, Efnisien threw him into the fire. Branwen-Ferch tried to jump into the fire to save him but was stopped.

There then began a great battle, but the Irish gained the advantage because they had the magic cauldron, and the dead Irish were being revived. Efnisien saw this and threw himself into the cauldron to destroy it, but he died in the act.

The battle then turned Bendigeidfran's way, and all the Irish warriors died. Bendigeidfran was pierced through the foot with a poison spear. Seven of his men were left alive, and he ordered them to cut off his head.

He instructed them to take his head to the white hill, in London, and place it facing France, so that his magic would protect Briton from attack.

The brother of Bendigeidfran, Manawydan, and some other men took the head of his brother and set off on the long journey to London. They passed by Harlech and went to the island of Grassholm, when the head began to talk to them. The men found this of great comfort, and they listened to the wisdom of the king. Yet when they were to continue their journey, a hundred years had passed. It was said that the feast of the wondrous head continued to amaze in the netherworld. Branwen-Ferch died of a broken heart.

There was a later reference to this legend, when the head of Llewellyn II head was decorated with ivy and positioned on the walls of the Tower of London for twelve years in the fourteenth century. The Tower of London was thought to have been built on the older White Tower, and this was seen as a slur against the Welsh, and their history.

I related this story because it is a myth, a legend, but it tells a story in the manner of the ancients, those tellers of our tales that carry a message and hold within them a moral. Whether any elements are true, we may never know. But it tells us too that there is a propensity to elaborate and weave into stories from that time some mystical elaborations.

I hope it will become clear to the reader that in this 'alternative' account of the life of Harold II we are considering, this is not the case.

What will become clear is that it is a simple story that has an honesty to which we all can relate.

Tostig, 1063

Let's continue. On Tostig's return to York, he found his treasury was much depleted. The support he'd given King Edward and his brother Harold in the campaign against the Welsh had cost him financially. He attempted to resolve this by raising the taxes across the whole of his domain. This did not sit well with the thegns and landowners of Northumbria.

In October 1065, while Tostig was visiting the king and his sister in the south, the disgruntled thegns marched on York, killed Tostig's men, and raided the treasury.

They then marched south to speak with Edward the confessor and demand that Tostig be removed. Their argument was the oppression they had suffered with high taxation along with the murders and torture of family members of some of the thegns and landowners. These were serious charges. Edward sent Harold Godwyn and his brothers to meet them.

By the time the northern thegns had reached Northampton, they had been joined by earls Morcar and Edwyn of Mercia. Harold met with them on their arrival at Oxford, and it was agreed that Morcar was to be the new earl, and they were to return to their families in the North because there still existed the threat of invasion from Scotland.

It appears that this was a decision Harold made without the sanction of the king, Edward.

It is speculation to read into this other motives that Harold may have had, but as we are observing these events, and those events that were to follow, we could venture a guess that a proposal had been made as an attempt to unite the families of Harold and Morcar and secure a suitable union for Harold should his rise to power continue.

Edith the Fair was to be advised by the royal advisors that Edith the Black, now widow of Gruffedd ap Llywelyn, was to be the new queen of the Saxon kingdom, and that an attempt should be made to impregnate her, leaving behind an heir for Harold.

It would be reasonable to presume that such arrangements were made with full disclosure to all parties that sanctioned and accepted that Edith the Black was the chip, although having placed this prospect before Harold, it seems he was open to an arrangement—not just because it was indeed an arrangement that would be to his advantage politically, but also because this Edith the Black, as she was known, was very beautiful in appearance. That is conjecture, I freely admit, and born more of my own mortal inclinations.

King Edward, who had angrily ordered Harold to take the army north, subdue these rebels, and reinstate Tostig, later changed his mind.

Tostig was incensed by what he saw as a betrayal first by his brother, whom he had fought alongside in the Welsh campaign, but also by his brother-in-law, the king. It was to be an act of outrageous depravity that was the undoing of Tostig and became the final straw, finally persuading the old king that Tostig had to leave England.

At a feast arranged in honour of King Edward by Harold, Tostig butchered Harold's servant, dismembering him, and served him up at the feast. It was the final straw and an event that saw the health of Edward decline. Edward agreed that Tostig should take some loyal thegns to Flanders with his wife, Judith, and stay with his brother-in-law, Baldwin, Duke of Flanders.

Furious at this seeming lack of loyalty from his own family, but also angry at his brother, whom he had supported in the tiring and costly Welsh campaign against Gruffydd ap Llywelyn, Tostig festered on this treachery while holed up in Flanders.

On 5 January 1066, Edward died and Harold became king.

It was reported that King Edward had serious doubts about passing the crown to Harold—not, strangely, because he felt Harold was not a fitting choice, for it was known that Harold had a royal lineage through the family of Alfred the Great, that of Alfred's eldest brother, who was himself (albeit briefly) king after Alfred's father. The doubts that plagued Edward were to do with a prophecy given to him by two monks in France many years before.

The Prophecy

During the month of January 1066, the holy king of England, St Edward the Confessor, was confined to his bed by his last illness in his royal Westminster Palace. St Aelred, Abbott of Rievaulx, in Yorkshire, relates that a short time before his happy death, this holy king was wrapped in ecstasy when two pious Benedictine monks of Normandy, whom he had known in his youth during his exile in that country, appeared to him and revealed to him what was to happen to England in future centuries—and the cause of the terrible punishment. They said, 'The extreme corruption and wickedness of the English nation has provoked the just anger of God. When malice shall have reached the fullness of its measure, God will, in His wrath, send to the English people wicked spirits who will punish and afflict them with great severity by separating the green tree from its parent stem the length of three furlongs. But at last this same tree, through the compassionate mercy of God, and without any national (governmental) assistance, shall return to its original root, reflourish, and bear abundant fruit.' After having heard these prophetic words, the saintly King Edward opened his eyes and returned to his senses, and the vision vanished. He immediately related all he had seen and heard to his virgin spouse, Edgitha; to Stigand, Archbishop of Canterbury; and to Harold, his successor to the throne, who was in his chamber praying around his bed.

These are the words Edward heard.

> The green tree which springs from the trunk
> When thence it shall be severed
> And removed to a distance of three acres
> By no engine or hand of man
> Shall return to its original trunk
> And shall join itself to its root
> Whence first it had origin
> The head shall receive again its verdure
> It shall bear fruit after its flower
> Then shall you be able for certainty
> To hope for amendment

It was said that with a heavy heart, Edward made known this prophecy to Harold and Archbishop Stigand, and he warned that the wickedness of William would come as retribution for the sins of the English and that in passing the crown to Harold, he was doing Harold no favours.

Harold himself was a true believer in signs and omens due to the experience he had when returning from the Welsh campaign and was afflicted with a form of paralysis. He prayed, it is said, before the holy cross and was cured. Harold surely would have taken to heart this sombre message, yet still he took on the role and, knowing the trouble to come, prepared his men for war.

Angered at his brother's rise to power, Tostig met with Duke William, the bastard of Normandy. His intention, which I doubt many would argue with, was to plot the downfall of his brother and seek his own prominence, his own triumphant return to England, his home, much as his father had done fourteen years before. By understanding how events unfolded at this time, we can see how plans played out, and deals were brokered.

Tostig travelled to Normandy to meet with William. He then crossed the channel and, with a small army, set about burning villages from the Isle of White moving up the coast and heading north. Such was the ferocity of these attacks that Earls Morcar and Edwyn sent men to confront Tostig at the Humber. Tostig fled to the protection of Malcolm III of Scotland. From here he travelled to engage the Norse king Hardrada in talks, aimed at persuading him to invade England and so gain the crown. This would have helped manoeuvre Tostig into a strong position and get back on his home turf.

Gaining Hardrada's trust was critical. But more critical was persuading him to cross with his armies and defeat his brother, Harold. He convinced Harald Hardrada that the Saxons in the North hated Harold and would join them, potentially doubling the size of his army.

Whether Hardrada was convinced is not known, but he was confident of his own army, undefeated over many battles, so he agreed. Having defeated the armies of the young earls Morcar and Edwyn at Fulford at the cost of over a thousand Saxon lives, Harald and Tostig moved on to York, taking control of the city. Had they stayed there, history may have been written differently.

After dividing his army, Harald took half his men to rest up at Stamford Bridge, allowing his men some time before continuing their campaign of conquest. Unknown to him, Harold and his housecarls rode north from London, picking up Frydmen on the way.

Harold, troubled by shooting pains in his right leg, is said to have had a vision of the impending battle, seeing his army as victorious. In eight days, Harold had moved a great army of Saxons two hundred miles, a bold but tiring move, yet he was still victorious. It is not clear who killed Tostig, yet his demise was not to be the end of his involvement in the great changes to the kingdom of the Saxons.

There is one account that tells of Harold facing his brother at Stamford Bridge, and in the company of the giant Viking king, Hardrada offered Tostig an earldom. When Tostig asked what Harold would give Hardrada, Harold replied, 'Seven feet of English soil, or as much as would see him buried in the ground.' Hardrada laughed and asked Tostig if this 'small man' was his brother. It was another slur because Harold was an impressive figure of over six feet, yet he was still smaller in height than Hardrada, who was said to have been closer to seven feet.

Tostig acknowledged Harold as his brother but was decapitated, it is said, by his brother Harold. This cannot be substantiated and remains unclear. Tostig had plotted well, and although he would not witness the results of his influence, the wheels of change were still turning.

William the Duke had landed on the south coast with a mighty army, and enough materials and skilled workers, to establish a fortified base in Crowhurst, near Pevensey. Surprise had been the winning formula for Harold's army against the Vikings at Stamford Bridge, yet this tactic was not to have success against William because he had outriders watching for Harold's approach.

I have found and confirmed information I believe to be accurate: that Harold's brother, Gurth, advised him to be cautious on this occasion and to rest up in London and wait for the support Harold would need to guarantee victory against William.

Something caused Harold to ignore this advice, but whether it was the reports of the brutal burning or the sacking of villages at Pevensey is unclear.

The killing of those people he had sworn to protect—those people he knew who lived on his land, loyal Englishmen and women true to him and, in the past, his father—must have troubled him. The knowledge that this troublesome duke of dubious birth had dared to challenge his right to the English throne must have spurred him on, but the truth is we will never know for sure.

Another possible explanation could be the Edward the Confessor prophecy. Was this behind Harold's anger and his determination to fight till death to beat back the bad omens that weighed him down? We know that for whatever reason, Harold took no advice and, after a brief rest for himself and his men, continued south to meet William, His intention? To drive William back into the sea.

The Question of an Oath

When I read through the Norman accounts of this period, I had to take care that I did not become drawn into too readily accepting likely propaganda that is passed down to us in the guise of accurately recorded histories of the time. There was the reporting on the sequence of events, and there were interpretations on how these events unfolded. For the most part, these were agreed upon, so we could say they are indisputable. Obviously, though, there was a politically driven agenda in the chronicles of the time. This we accept.

On looking back on those times, I felt strongly that there was inevitably a need for me to look closely at the known information of the time and what was reported.

I felt I had to examine the histories and engage in some reading between the lines. If we look, for example, at the deaths of prominent figures on the field of battle in similar conflicts contemporary to the conflict at Hastings, there were Stamford Bridge, with Harald Hardrada and Tostig. Both bodies were found, even though it had been reported that the battle caused the death of thousands and piles of bodies were just abandoned, left to rot where they fell, for years after.

Hardrada was found and given a full burial in his homeland. Tostig was transferred and buried in York, even though his head had been removed and, it could be said (as has been said of Harold), that he was not deserving of such reverence.

According to the history books, Harold and his brother Gurth were killed on Senlac Hill, yet confusion and doubts surround this assumption, as we have found.

In searching for more understanding about our ancient histories, we are sometimes helped along that path with little gifts, offerings from the faceless and sometimes nameless archivists who in times past wrote addenda as an insight into their own personal understanding of those accounts, when the balance between truthfulness and deceit had to be compromised.

Very often I found their conclusions include a note that contradicts their own written and perceived historical truth, but rather than confuse the reader, it will clarify an account or a statement and transform the focus of our attention at that time by adding a most valuable piece of the jigsaw.

I'll wager that there are few historians, educated in the higher echelons of our hallowed halls of learning, who can, with hand on heart, declare that they are open and willing to take a fresh look at an established norm in terms of their journey of education. Few are those who can accept a new thought without this new, proposed thought causing heartburn or some other digestive disturbance.

However, if you are a protagonist by nature, you become the holder of the baton. You have the freedom to delve and probe and scrape away the grime and dust that had confined the light of truth to a pitiful, faint glow over the centuries.

Perjurer?

If we are to give serious consideration to the accusation thrown at King Harold after his defeat in 1066—that he was a perjurer, and that he had sworn over ancient relics to give the throne to William when Edward died—we must view this assumption and this testimony with caution. It is not constructive, offering an assumption on sections of our history that have already been accepted as most likely simply because it has been accepted as so over many seminars, lectures, and so forth—unless, of course it is more than an assumption.

The Anglo-Saxon Chronicles has always been the last word on events in this period in our history. This is a good point of reference, and as we look through the *Chronicles*, we find no mention of Harold's journey over to France. This must flag some concerns, because this accusation formed the basis of a legal case against Harold and was, in effect, the holy nail that was hammered into the front door of Pope Alexander, on which he hung his flag of support for a low-born duke, to attack a legitimate sovereign and the kingdom of England.

The Anglo-Saxon Chronicles was written for the purpose of recording the legal history of the Saxons; in other words, it recorded all the important matters of state as it happened, and more important, these events were written as these events became known.

If Harold had travelled to France and had sworn to give the throne to William—two years before Edward even became ill, and before other heirs had been discounted—why was it not included in *The Anglo-Saxon Chronicles*? It begs the question, 'Did this event happen?'

This I will cover later.

We are not unaccustomed to the effects of propaganda, and even as recently as this yet young century we live in, we have already witnessed how a leader of a nation can be accused of a diabolical act so plausible as to cause an invasion of his country and the destruction of his kingdom, only to learn too late that what was said was lies, for there were no weapons of mass destruction. If enough people in power say it, the people will believe it. It is that simple, and that twisted.

CHAPTER 2

The Battle of Hastings, 1066

Many of us remember drawing in class Norman and Saxon shields with various colourful designs for a history project. The battle scene with the two opposing armies lined up in formation was a part of our school curriculum, our history.

The year was 1066. It was 13 October, the night before the battle, and the emissaries from both camps had conveyed their thoughts to each leader in the slim hope of battle being avoided, It was not to be.

It has been estimated that after the swift march south by Harold, the king of the English, that the numbers in the Saxon camp had diminished somewhat. The Norman force of fighting men was estimated at around seven to ten thousand men, and although Harold's number was said to be much less than that, there was a difference in the tactics employed on the day, and it was to unfold as battle commenced how strategy was to be the deciding factor in determining who won that day, not just might or commitment.

Harold had chosen the better vantage position, at the top of Senlac Hill. However, the area to defend was restricted, meaning that there were only so many places to fill for the shield wall. This meant that actual fighting men, able to participate and be affective, was reduced.

Therefore even though the Saxons had the high ground, the effectiveness of William's army had almost doubled by the time the battle was set to commence the following day.

Harold's force was around six thousand, yet only around half that number were strategically placed to engage the enemy. Harold was outnumbered.

On 14 October, the battle lines were set, and the Saxon shield wall was in place.

There now followed the prebattle stand-off before hostilities commenced. Shouting, 'Out, out,' against the invaders, Saxons would have slammed their axes and swords against their shields to a drum-like beat, and the French, Normans, and Bretons would have shouted back.

It is possible too that the Saxons would have heard of the slaughter of the town of Crowhurst and, in the distance, the destruction of fellow Saxons' small holdings, adding to their anger. The battle throughout the day was a series of varied assaults by both Normans and Bretons trying to break through the Saxon wall. Knights on horseback, in groups of fifteen or so, attempted to break through. Then archers were used, followed by groups of Bretons on foot. These were occupied to the far right of the Saxon wall, attacking different places along the shield wall, and these would prove to be the key to unlocking the stalemate on the day.

It was late afternoon when William instructed the archers to fire high so that the arrows fell onto the Saxons from a great hight. This tactic had some success. To the right of where Harold stood, behind the shield wall, a group of Fyrdmen watched as the group of Bretons who had tried to break through the shield wall turned tail and ran away, and as some fell, the Fyrdmen chased after them as they feigned retreat back down the hill. The shield wall broke ranks. Many Saxons believed that the battle was turning. This weakened the defences of the Saxons.

The daylight was beginning to fade, and once again archers were employed, as they had been throughout the day. Harold was caught in the eye. Angrily, Harold removed the arrow and snapped it in two, throwing it away as he rested on his shield.

With the pain so great, Harold was momentarily unable to fight on, and upon seeing Harold slumped on his shield, the Norman knights who had assaulted the shield wall in small groups after the archers' assault sent up a great shout and pushed on to break through the shield wall. Finally they succeeded in breaking the shield wall.

Harold had fallen, and after a brutally long day of conflict, it was the first chance William's army had of victory.

I will refer back to the events at this moment because they are critical in understanding how the real truth about the life of Harold and his brother, Gurth, was to unfold.

The chronicler for Master Wace records something interesting at this point. I ask the reader to remember this; the reason why will become clear later. He reports that Gurth had seen the Norman knights break through from his position on Harold's right flank. He saw that Harold had, amazingly, re-engaged the enemy but that Harold could see very little. Gurth moved quickly to be at his brother's side when Gurth himself was struck a mighty blow and was felled to the ground.

It was then that Harold too was struck by a sword on his ventaille (the protective mail around his helmet), knocking him to the ground. There was a second blow as he tried to raise himself. A knight on horseback rode over him and cut through his thigh, down to the bone.

As the knights on horseback drove through the battle lines of the Saxons, upon seeing Harold fallen, some Saxons began to back away.

As the Norman army pushed on, the fighting, which was still fierce, moved away from the top of Senlac Hill and on towards the Mal Fosse. This was a wooded and deep ravine behind the hill that was planned as a last place of retreat for the Saxon army, because it was treacherous for knights on horseback and made full-on hand-to-hand fighting difficult.

This was where many Norman knights perished, and many of the retreating Saxons managed to fade into the growing darkness.

This was Hastings in 1066. History was made, and William became the new king of the English. Although this was a time we would struggle to understand in our modern, civilised world, for a conquest to be considered legitimate, the laws and politics of the day dictated a need to justify an action of one country against another, particularly if both nations were Christian.

What 'justification' did William have to invade the sovereign state of England? Who had more right to the throne of England? Many have argued that Harold was a usurper, a dishonest man. Many say William had more right. What is the truth?

Duke William

William was the illegitimate son of Duke Robert I of Normandy; his mother, Arlette, was a tanner's daughter. He was connected to Edward, and royalty in England, only by an in-law relative who was a female consort. Harold had a stronger, unbroken male line of descent from the older brother of King Alfred, King Aethelred the Elder. Also, he was elected duly by the Witan and sanctioned by Edward the Confessor.

I feel some nefarious skulduggery has been at work in preserving the lineage of some of our characters of note. It seems strange to me that with most families whose history is preserved, it is not often that lineage is lost or doubts are cast on the nobility. However, in the case of King Harold II, and with the obvious bias shown his family by the Norman propaganda machine, it is little wonder I struggled to nail down the lineage of Harold and had to look to Northern Europe to find the full list of his descendants from the royal line of Wessex.

The Line of Harold from Aethelred I, King of Wessex

Aethelheim, 848-898, son of Aethelred I, King of Wessex
Father to
Aethelfrith, Earl of Mercia, 870–927
Father to
Eadric, Earl of Wessex, 920–949
Father to
Aethelweard, Thegn of Sussex (the historian), d. 998
Father to
Aethelmar Cild, 960–1015
Father to
Wulfnoth Cild, Earl of Sussex, 983–1014

Father to
Godwyn, Earl of Wessex, 1001–1053
Father to
King Harold II, 1022–1112

How William Secured the Support of Pope Alexander II

In the spring of 1066, William asked for the blessing of the pope in return for his support. Although it was not permitted for the church to give support to one Christian country against another, the papal banner was sent to William. This concession was politically motivated and was not sanctioned by the rest of the synod.

After understanding the overwhelming support William had gained for this campaign, and the likely allies the Norman Duke would gain from the success of this conquest, it was clear that William would be able to command a great army afterwards. The pope needed military aid for his own campaigns in the east.

After the battle in 1066, when the battle had been won, there was an allegation against Harold: in 1064, Harold had sworn on holy relics that should King Edward die, then Harold would support William as the new King of England. Harold was posthumously accused of being a perjurer. How this supposed meeting came about has raised doubts.

One account says that Harold was engaged in a fishing trip, and his boat was blown off course in the English Channel. He was saved by Frenchmen at Ponthieu, and then after Guy of Ponthieu imprisoned Harold, William secured his release. Harold then joined William on one of his campaigns, where Harold heroically saved two of William's men from being lost in quicksand. It is said Harold formed an attachment to the daughter of William, Adeliza, who was seven at the time.

Harold, who had his own navy and who was a skilled seaman, being so lost at sea while fishing and ending up in Ponthieu does not make sense. As for the location for this act of swearing on holy relics, for such a significant event, this was an act of 'tricking' Harold into giving his support to William, a Norman!

That none of the chroniclers can agree not only where this took place but also when raises concerns. This whole story is supposed to have been squeezed into a pretty tight time frame, where we have Harold on a very arduous campaign just a few months before, fighting the Welsh king with his brother Tostig, going from South Wales to the North, sailing his fleet to meet up with Tostig, who had begun his campaign into Wales from the West near Chester. All this is recorded in detail in *The Anglo-Saxon*

Chronicles, then, because the Welsh king is murdered in Snowdonia later in the year and deals for lands, and self-rulership with vassalship is discussed. Then Harold is supposed to nip off for a bit of fishing, suffers a serious misjudgement in naval terms, is blown 130 miles off course, and is easily captured by some Frenchmen. He then is lavishly entertained, given gifts, offered William's seven-year-old daughter as a future wife, and joins William on a military campaign into Brittany for several months? And on their return, William demands Harold swear on a box of relics?

Let's look at the record all historians use as the foremost authority on our history when examining Anglo-Saxon history, *The Anglo-Saxon Chronicles*. It tells us that after the Welsh rebellion, Harold was engaged in the work of organising the building of a structure in the place he had just conquered, South Wales, in order to hold a hunting party later. The date of these celebrations? It was 1065, and Edward sought to enjoy, as a way of marking that important time, the successful campaign against the Welsh king Gruffydd.

This was in a time where travel took time and when, instead of resting up after such an arduous campaign, Harold was said to have headed east during the preparations for the celebrations for the king and gone to France.

There is no mention in *The Anglo-Saxon Chronicles* of any trip to France, accident or otherwise. This story came to light in 1066, and the first ever mention of relics being sworn over was in the Bayeux Tapestry. An event of such legal and political significance as a senior earl so close to the king of England swearing on holy relics not being mentioned in *The Anglo-Saxon Chronicles* is not possible. This supposed event, being so politically significant, would most definitely have been entered into the Anglo-Saxon histories.

I remember being involved as chief bricklayer in St Albans on a very prestigious site, building two villas under the scrutiny of Kevin McCloud and his TV people for a chap called Chris. Thinking back, I wondered if it ever occurred to me that I should up and leave this project and sail off for a few months. That would never happen. I had some help from another bricklayer, but I had eighteen thousand bricks to lay, and not in a traditional way. It required my daily attention because other trades relied on my progress.

I cannot get my head around how, after having fought such an arduous campaign, and just when he was in the middle of building a prestigious hall for his king, he would clear off on some trip to France for fishing, then stay in France for most of that year, when the grand hall he was supposed to be having made was being attacked by the Welsh and his people were being killed.

This event was not reported on or recorded at the time. There was not even a whisper of this before the battle, and most important, it was not entered into the records that contained all information that was of national interest, *The Anglo-Saxon Chronicles*. It cannot be considered a legitimate accusation against the rightfully elected king, Harold II.

It is unlikely that Harold travelled to France in 1064 and swore allegiance to William. There are some scholars who suggest that a visit did take place, but it was viewed by King Edward as a risky move. It raises an interesting supposition. If this trip did occur and Edward had warned Harold, as the Bayeux Tapestry seems to indicate (see the depiction of Edward's raised finger to Harold, before Harold's departure), to be careful of William's tricky nature, then it would add weight to the argument that Harold and Edward were on good terms. This would make sense, looking at the overall picture from this perspective. The argument would hold true that Edward saw Harold as his loyal subject and not a potential usurper.

Harold had served the king loyally, had quelled rebellions in the North, and had sealed a peace deal with the Welsh. The kingdom was in safe hands, so it would seem that Edward had no intention of leaving the rulership of England to William.

Holy Relics

Postconquest England, there was so much unrest over the Norman invasion. William needed to be viewed as a legitimate king, and the church wielded great influence over the people. How was William to convince the people that his claim was a legitimate claim on the English throne? Could he declare that Harold was an oath breaker?

There is a strong case for us concluding that either William lied to convince the pope that Harold was an oath breaker (see William's deathbed confession), or a deal was struck between the pope and William.

Aside from the military support the pope needed, he could have added an agreement for the construction of more churches and cathedrals, as well as more control of what was a sloppy, uncooperative nation of Saxons who were always casual about their sense of priority when it came to loyalty to the church in Rome.

If the church under Saxon rule, preconquest, was really as described by William of Malmesbury in 1135, 'Run by ignorant Bishops like Archbishop Stigand, and badly in need of reform', then there is no doubt this change would have suited the pope and William. They simply needed to have an honourable excuse to invade.

However, the pope thought he was to benefit from the conquest in terms of a more profitable England from the church's point of view. Alexander II did not get the military support he was promised from William. So was William an oath breaker? Surely not.

I want to address another suggestion put forward by historians: that Harold decided to travel to France to secure the release of his brother, Wulfnoth, and his nephew, Hakon. This is another supposition I have tried to get to the bottom of. There are puzzling elements to this story, and there is conflicting evidence. Eadmer (1066–1126) wrote that Wulfnoth, the young son of Earl Godwineson, was a hostage in the castle of William I. How did he become a hostage?

It Is believed

I have noticed that when repeating this story, often these phrases are attached to it: 'It is believed', 'It is thought', and 'Some say'. From the research I have carried out, there is a tendency to accept a story as likely true, without checking whether the information stands up to examination. There are reasons why and how this story came about after the Norman Conquest, I believe. This goes back again to the manipulating of minds and hearts of the time. If a story is to have real conviction, it has to be watertight.

I believe that the Norman propaganda machine began in earnest immediately after the battle. After all the earls and nobles had been rounded up and sent over to Normandy, these stories became widespread. Without a doubt, the most necessary and important of all these stories was to be the swearing of an oath over an amassed pile of hidden, holy relics. Why? Because it legitimised the invasion in the eyes of the church, and of the people.

This is the story. Harold was sent to William in 1064 to plead for the return of both Wulfnoth, his younger brother, and Hakon, his nephew. Another story is that Harold went fishing, and his boat got blown off course. Harold was captured. William, the good, straight and true Christian duke, saved Harold, and they became friends.

The story continues. Harold saved two of William's men, and they all got on famously, but as Harold tried to negotiate the release of Wulfnoth and Hakon, only Hakon was released. Then Harold was made to swear an oath that he would support William as the next king of England. Harold swore it and then was shown the holy relics. He returned to England.

The question is, Why was it necessary for it to be recorded in all the Norman chronicles that Harold did this two years before the conflict, and in a particular year where, in *The Anglo-Saxon Chronicles*, it was a 'blank' year—in other words, it was the year after Harold and Tostig's exhausting campaign in the West, where they had been engaged in a brutal war against the Welsh king, Gruffydd-ap- Llewelyn.

And it was before that equally eventful year during which Tostig was sacked, Harold made peace with Earls Morcar and Edwyn, a marriage, and a revolt in the North.

So, a gap year in the well-respected recordings of Saxon history, *The Anglo-Saxon Chronicles* was a convenient year to pick out. Looking at this all with an understandably suspicious eye, I can't help but feel the Normans lied to us—a lot.

So when was this hostage taking of Wulfnoth and Hakon said to have happened?

Notes on the lies and meddling by the French church in the politics of England, and the trouble this caused between King Edward and the old earl, Godwyn.

Histories record that it was believed the French bishop Archbishop Robert fled England, taking the two young Godwyns, Hakon and Wulfnoth, as hostages, in 1051. Again we look to *The Anglo-Saxon Chronicles* for clarity. For the French archbishop, it is clear from the tone of the Anglo-Saxon account that once the misunderstanding between the Godwyns and the king were cleared up, the archbishop and his French associates fled in panic and in fear for their lives. The fleeing is described as on horseback and fighting their way through London to finally escape by boat, back to France.

There is no mention of them stopping off to pick up the two Godwyns, Hakon and Wulfnoth, kidnapping them while engaged in swordplay as they maimed and killed young Englishmen in their attempt to flee.

We also gain some more insight here of the lies told to the king by the French about the intentions of the old Earl Godwyn, and how these lies were exposed. Later, lies about Harold due to the successful invasion were not exposed, and we are beginning to understand how devious the French were in concocting false stories to elevate themselves and justify an invasion.

What follows is a section taken from *The Anglo-Saxon Chronicles* in reference to that period when Archbishop Robert fled England after his lies had been exposed.

CHAPTER 3

The Vita Haroldi. To introduce this extraordinary document, I first would like to explain its background. It was written as part of a rebuttal, and I found this interesting. In his historical work, *Castles and Abbeys of England*, William Beattie describes a serious rift in the church at Waltham after the battle, where some of those in high positions within the church argued over the conflicting stories as to what happened to their king, Harold, after the battle. It seems that this disagreement was not satisfactorily resolved, and William Beattie explains that both groups went away to record their own version of events. This manuscript, which has come to be known by researchers and historians as the Harleian MS 3773, is now more widely known as The Vita Haroldi.

It was kept in the sole, safe keeping of the Church at Waltham, of whom King Harold was a beloved patron, for four hundred years. Since its discovery by those outside of the Church at Waltham in the early nineteenth century, it has been referred to as 'The romance of the life of Harold, King of England'. It tells the story of Harold being carried at night, close to death, from the battlefield in 1066—and being healed. Then it discusses Harold living as a pilgrim on the road, travelling in Europe and possibly the holy land, before returning to England to die in Chester after a long life.

William of Malmesbury

To understand why this work is not taken seriously by most historians today, I will bring in the first witness, the writer of the alleged myth and my first swipe at the widely accepted and adopted authority on the subject of the Norman Conquest, the renowned William of Malmesbury.

William of Malmesbury wrote that Harold died on Senlac Hill in 1066. William was half Norman and was said to have travelled up and down the country collecting information for his historical collection of writings. It is said that William was meticulous in his research and was trusted and respected as a historian.

What did he know? Why did the monk at Waltham who copied the testimony of Andrew, the young priest who took Harold's last confession as recorded in the Vita Haroldi, call William of Malmesbury a dishonest man and a perjurer? Was there a private conversation between William and the brothers at Waltham? Was William made aware of Harold's surviving? Did he decide, in view of the unanimity among his own people and from so many other chroniclers of the time, to go with the politically safer view that Harold had died? Or was the reference to do with the accusation that Harold was a perjurer?

One more question is raised, and I think it is a very important question. Was there a medieval gag order placed on the writer of the Vita Haroldi back in those times, when this news of Harold's escape could have been a financial problem for the Abbey at Waltham? Of course, we cannot know this; we can simply surmise from the 'unspoken words' in the text of the Vita Haroldi. But let us ruminate for just a moment.

In 1847, William Beattie was looking through the available histories of the time, and he describes a row amongst senior members at the abbey. It is easy to understand how this exchange could have taken place, yet everyone back then would have quickly understood the need for caution. There had to be a political solution as the revealing of news that Harold had escaped. Firstly, it put Harold's life in danger, and he was their patron.

Also, care had to be taken when it came to disrupting the steady flow of contributions made to the abbey by those pilgrims and visitors who travelled far to visit the last resting place of King Harold. Political and financial ramifications needed to be considered, and a resolution was quickly reached.

This was done by each camp being told to write their own versions of this dispute. As we know, the 'truth' chosen was the financially and politically correct one. Harold had died, and Edith, his handfasted wife, had identified Harold's body by the 'markings' only she would know about on his body.

I personally believe there is some truth in the unknown monk's testimonies against William of Malmsbury. After all, why would a half Norman, living comfortably within a Norman oligarchy, ruffle feathers? Would he not rather desire to retain the status quo?

Harold's Death, and the Absence of a Body

Let's look at the immediate aftermath of a bloody battle and ask questions like, Who would know the whereabouts of a king? How many soldiers died instantly during the battle? How many were so badly wounded that they died through loss of blood sometime afterwards?

As was recorded by Master Wace in reference to Harold and his younger brother Gurth, 'Gurth moved across to his brother, but was felled and did not rise again'. Therefore we have eyewitness testimony that Gurth and Harold had fallen not far from each other, it was growing dark, and the battle had quickly moved away, beyond the brow of the hill that the Saxons had held all that day. No more is said of Harold and Gurth until it was stated that it had been recorded that Harold's body was found, and he was buried.

Let's go back to that point in the battle, after Gurth and Harold fell. It's recorded that the battle did not end at the falling of Harold, and Harold was said to have fallen as it was growing dark. The battle continued into the night because it was by no means over. I wanted to give thought to this and those hours of dark, sometime after all the fighting ceased, when it would have been safe for locals to search amongst the dead. What wounds inflicted would have been life-threatening? We can learn this from the testimonies of Master Wace.

He writes, 'Harold was struck in the eye with an arrow.' This was clearly not a 'death stroke', as has been suggested, because Harold was seen to pull out the arrow, snap it, and angrily throw it away. It is unclear how much time elapsed from Harold's losing his eye and the final assault that ended his fight. It was reported that he fought on although in great pain.

He then was struck on his ventaille (face mask) and fell under the blow. As he tried to rise, a knight struck his thigh down to the bone, and no more was recorded of Harold, only that he had died.

There have been exaggerated claims that a group of Norman knights butchered the remains of Harold, cutting off his head and carrying away a severed limb. Really? We would struggle to understand the manner and brutality of hand-to-hand combat in those times.

The housecarls who stood with Harold and fought alongside him were particularly ferocious fighters, greatly respected by those professional soldiers who fought for William.

When the shield wall would collapse in a battle situation, a Saxon housecarl had two leather straps at the back of his shield, and he would hang the round shield around his neck, take his sword and axe, and attack and defend with both arms, wearing the shield like a large, round breastplate. These soldiers were strong, professional fighting men, said to be powerful enough to bring down horse and rider with one stroke, and these horses were large beasts. Would you waste energy butchering a fallen warrior who was no longer an immediate threat, and not forgetting the mutual respect these professionals had for one another?

The Question of a Body Gone Missing

During the battle, it was recorded that both William and Harold were identified quite noticeably. William, seen to have been unseated from his horse and given a new one, raised his helmet to reveal to his troops that he was still alive. Harold, a powerful and tall soldier, was seen dispatching all before him in the thick of battle with his standard nearby, before being struck in the eye, resting on his shield, and attempting to rally before being cut down by Norman knights and ridden over.

Holmfirth, West Yorkshire, 1975

When I read the testimony given to Master Wace, I remembered something from my training to become a stone mason. I witnessed an old mason whose sharp chisel had sprung back out of a fissure in a piece of stone and pierced his eye. He had made a cardinal error: he had released his grip on the chisel with his left hand and given the chisel a mighty blow with his lump hammer. The sharp chisel had sunk deep in his eye, and he closed both eyes because of the pain. All he could do was sit holding his hands over his face as blood ran between his fingers.

The injury did not kill him, but he lost his eye.

This description of Harold having to rest on his shield and the mason's pain was obvious to me, I can only imagine the pain. He was unable to do any more work, and he could no longer see out of either eye due to the pain.

In the account of Master Wace, it tells us that Harold rested on his shield and then rose again to fight on, defending himself from the Norman knight on horseback. Harold was felled by blows to his ventaille and a serious wound to his thigh. Having seen how debilitating losing an eye can be, I can only conclude that this was war, and I am left to reflect on the possible scene of a determined and powerful man who overcame great pain to continue fighting. This is testament to the stature of these warriors.

I have used the writings of Master Wace as a reference in this work on more than one occasion, though not because he favours the direction of my research. I will explain briefly why, out of all those who wrote histories on the Norman Conquest, I lean a little more towards Master Wace. There has been new evidence that has recently come to light in relation to the invasion that has not been known since medieval times.

In the times of the early Victorians, when serious attention was given to history, it was widely thought that the works of Master Wace, having been examined closely, lacked accuracy and had many mistakes as to geographic locations and details surrounding the actual invasion. Therefore, his testimony was not seriously considered.

Recently, archaeologists have looked again at the description given by Master Wace, including his description of the inland sea of Pevensey and the area of Crowhurst. Because of their findings, historians have now elevated the works of Master Wace as one of the most accurate accounts of those times.

From my study of his other records on this subject, I have to agree. Where I disagree with Master Wace are his personal observations that are clearly prejudiced, as well as those histories that were not from eyewitness testimony, but presumed. In these, he follows the general trend of the time. Therefore, I want to look again at those hours after the battle.

CHAPTER 4

The Following Day

Would it really have been so hard to find such a figure, even if those Normans who, in the thick of the heaviest fighting against swinging axes and swords, would have felt compelled to cut up and butcher the lifeless body of Harold?

Imagine you were there, fighting for your land and your life. You are a Norman trying to push back a mass of angry Saxons on their land. It is late in the day, and you have been wielding a sword that by this time must feel three times the weight. Would you pause to butcher a fallen soldier who was no longer able to defend himself? Or, as a professional soldier, would you push on while you had the strength to finish off the real threat that was still before you—angry Saxons wielding axes and swinging swords?

Remembering too that the light of the day was fading; on 14 October, it is dusk by 6 p.m. It was said to have been around dusk when Harold finally fell. The Normans were on the very threshold of a victory, and many must have wondered whether it would actually happen.

Would they pause, even for a few moments, over a fallen king and risk the regrouping of the Saxons overnight? Add to this the news of the ships said to have been sent to cut off William's escape back to Normandy if his attempts at invading England had failed.

Waltham Abbey

There was a conversation between the sacristan of Waltham and the two senior canons, Osegode Cnoppe and Ailric Childemaister, as they voiced their concerns over the bad omens they had witnessed. This incident is worth looking at again.

Harold had bowed before the holy cross on the morning of his departure, on his way first to London and then on to meet William at Hastings.

The sacristan felt sure he had witnessed the 'wooden head' of the image bow in a sad fashion towards Harold. This was interpreted by him as being a sad omen—that Harold would not gain the victory in the coming battle. It was this fear that prompted all three to agree that Osegode and Ailric should accompany Harold and his army so that should Harold fall, the two of them could retrieve the body and return to the abbey with Harold, and their patron could be interned with dignity at his own church.

These two senior canons were, I have no doubt, at the battle throughout the day, intent on the actions of their king and patron. They were willing him to survive and win the day.

It is inconceivable that they would not have stuck loyally to their task, looking constantly for the tall figure of Harold at the highest point on Senlac Hill and marking the spot where he fell as dark descended. They also would have been concerned that they should not become caught up in the battle themselves, knowing at the time that it was not unheard of for monks to fight; patriotic to the cause, they would certainty have picked up axe and sword to join the fray.

As darkness descended and the ferocious fighting moved into the Mal-Fosse and farther on to the mashes and the now-fabled wooden bridge, where many more were said to have died, would not Osegode and Ailric have been waiting through that night for the calmness and the quiet, when all activities had ceased and the soldiers of William had at last taken some long overdue rest? Surely in the first light of the new day, Sunday, was when they could agree once more to venture forth onto the battlefield strewn with the dead and dying and seek out Harold, before the bodies were stripped of their mail coats and tunics. I guess that they would, already with the last position they had witnessed Harold making his final stand marked firmly in their memory. They would have headed for that place to find Harold.

We know from the records at the church that they could not find him. Could they have maybe not looked hard enough? Was it not their only sacred task that day of battle to mark the exact spot where Harold fell for the purpose of finding and returning him to Waltham?

There were others that day who searched for their family or those with some life in them, yet Harold could not be found. Yet somehow the journey back to Waltham from the battlefield at Senlac Hill was to take them three days. What a puzzle it must have been for them to have misplaced their patron. After all, there were some obvious distinguishing features about Harold that would still have been about him so soon after the battle. The royal hauberk would be one, visibly superior to other chain mail. These two canons were very familiar with Harold's other features and distinguishing marks. It is a puzzle to me that if this one task was their sole reason for travelling so far, how did they fail?

It was reported later they heard another story—heresy at the time—that a local woman and her two sons, had found Harold still in life in those hours of darkness, as Osegode and Ailric slept, and carried him to safety to Winchester. Was this why they could not find Harold on that cold Sunday morning?

Why, then, did these same canons from Waltham have to persuade Edith the Fair to accompany them back to the battlefield to identify Harold's body? One report said she was with the other wives, behind the lines during the battle, as was the custom at such important events, cooking and caring for the injured. (Edith the Raven, Harold's queen, was not there because she was heavily pregnant and intent on protecting her unborn child, the future heir to the throne.)

Whether this was true or not—that Edith the Fair was seen by the apple tree, close to the battle—we will never know. Would she have fallen out with her husband for marrying another Edith, even if she had understood and accepted that there were political benefits to be gained from the union? They were together many years, and I can understand if she was there or not there.

But if she had been there, and if she had been forced away by the intensity of the battle that day, would she not return the following day to see whether Harold was dead? In balance, and from the actions and conversations that were had between the canons and the sacristan, it seems unlikely that Edith was there.

Was there another reason why these same canons, Osegode and Ailric, having travelled all the way back from the battle without Harold, would have argued for returning on what to them would surely have been a fruitless task? What odds would they have given themselves of finding the body, even with Edith this time? By now, after so long—it being at the very least a four-week interlude—the bodies would be naked, swollen, and decayed.

Looking at the argument that clearly split the church at Waltham at the time, is it possible that the brothers at Waltham needed to provide a body as a symbol, for the people to visit and say prayers over? The body would act as a focus and a location for pilgrims to visit and pay homage to. It was stated in the histories of the church that the return of Edith, with the 'body' of her husband, identified by the secret marks only she would know of from their long history of intimacy, was well publicised, and many thousands gathered at the bridge on her return and gave thanks and praises, along with much sorrowing, on the return of their king and patron.

It was also recorded later that the brother of Harold visited the church, looked down at the body said to be his brother, and remarked, 'You may have some fellow here, but it is not my brother.' This event has been argued over for many years. Was it really Harold's brother? When was this? Was this simply too long after to accept that one of Harold's brothers could still be alive? What did this relative know?

The thing to remember is when entries into the histories of the church at Waltham were made, we who examine and criticise these were simply not there! There are events written about during those times that were clearly 'of a certain time'. The people who wrote these histories did not always make themselves known. Some histories go back further than others, but because these were all legitimate recordings that were pertinent to the church, they were included.

In the case of Gyrth, the brother of Harold, we have evidence that he survived the battle and spoke with Henry I at Woodstock in the year 1125. This is accepting, as is noted in the Latin text where this appeared, that by this time Gyrth was of an extraordinary age and living in a hermitage near Oxford. From what we can deduce from the records, he would have been 90 years old. Quite an age. We do not know when Gyrth spoke to the fathers at Waltham when declaring to them that the body they thought was Harold was in fact not! I would like to surmise that this meeting was close in time to the other meeting at Woodstock. The reason for this is these are the only two occasions we have come across when Gyrth made himself known. It seems that for the rest of his life, he kept his identity quite secret. It could possibly be that his arrival at Waltham could well have been directly before or just after his being at Woodstock. That would logically mean that event can be approximately dated at around 1125. I suggest this because of the description given of Gyrth on both of these occasions, which are very much the same: 'tall in stature elegant, though of a great age, and dressed as a Hermit'. More on this later, but my thoughts on this are that the recording of this event should not be so quickly discounted.

Harold's Injuries

There is the question of the left eye damage. The events of that day, as recorded by the chroniclers of the twelfth century, had to rely on the testimony of others, and even more so the testimonies of the testimonies of those they could find who remembered those events.

Putting this into some form of context we may be able to relate to is like when I asked my uncle about the experiences my grandfather went through in the trenches. As time passes, the opportunity to gather eyewitness accounts fades.

The eyewitness from the battle who spoke to the father of Master Wace, who then spoke to his son of the battle, said that Harold was seen to have been struck in his right eye. He then pulled it out angrily and snapped the arrow before sinking to his knees and resting on his shield momentarily because of the pain. Yet all reports of Harold as a pilgrim and then a hermit say that his left eye was lost! Could the eyewitness have been talking of the right side, from his perspective, looking front on at the battle lines of the Saxons?

Harold's Burial

For the historical commentators throughout the centuries since the battle, there has been another problem: the body of Harold—or the lack of it. It has always been accepted that Harold died at Hastings, and it's easy to see why. His survival would have been a well-kept secret for many years, and although the body was never found, it was generally accepted that he died on the battlefield.

It's true that anyone can dispute this claim and say he survived, but in order to seriously challenge established history, you need proof, so it remains true in regard to this question of Harold's death. Without a body, how can we know?

What we can do, while we are awaiting the exhumation of the unmarked grave we have discovered at Waltham, is examine closely the arguments from both sides.

There is nothing to dispute, no argument from either point of view up to that moment, where Harold is felled and trampled on, because slain and wounded alike fell around and on him from both armies. Most versions of the story agree. Where it gets interesting is in the hours after nightfall. The battle had moved swiftly on into the night as Saxons lost ground and Normans sought to end the conflict, away from where Harold fell, moving on into the Mal Fosse or ravine where so many Norman knights and their horses died, lured in by the retreating Saxons.

We have looked at the responsibility given to Osegode and Ailric, and we have given thought to what was likely seen the following morning as a simple task: returning to the place where Harold fell and recovering his body for burial. But apparently it was not simple.

The various chroniclers of the time have written different stories. One stated that Harold's body parts were wrapped in purple and delivered to William. This would have been observed by the two Waltham canons and reported back to Waltham. Another stated that Edith was escorted to the battlefield some weeks later to identify Harold by certain marks. There was obviously a problem that morning, because immediately after the battle, Gytha, Harold's mother, asked for the body from William. Why? And why did she offer William Harold's body weight in gold? Had she and her people looked for Harold but not found him where he was said to have fallen?

This is worth consideration, because now we have not only Osegode and Ailric desperately trying to find Harold but also Gytha and her people. Again we ask, Why could nobody find him?

What we do know is that there was a concern the body could not be found and identified, and three weeks later, the fathers at Waltham had to convince Edith it was necessary for her to go back with them to find the dead Harold. Another scenario is also possible: they needed to find any body that they could have identified as Harold, in order that this missing body conundrum could be resolved and the body could be buried, so it would be visited and revered in order to appease the people of Waltham.

There are other variations on the whereabouts of his body.

1. Buried at sea.
2. On the beachhead overlooking the sea.
3. Burned in a Viking-style funeral.
4. Taken by Gytha, his mother, to be buried at Waltham.
5. Buried at Stansted Abbots or Bosham.
6. Taken by Edith the Fair after she identified his body by certain marks to Waltham.

Let's add one more, the English version: he was found alive in the early hours and ferried to Winchester by his people to be secretly healed by a skilled nurse from Spain.

To view the evidence for and against his having died at Hastings, and to do so without prejudice, I thought it important to look at all the evidence with an open mind. The tendency is to believe the history we have grown up with, the history taught and accepted in our schools and colleges. What is dishonest is to label information that's new or different as improbable, unlikely, a myth, or a fancy without looking at these findings. This is why this research and my findings will be difficult for most historians, because they already see the hermit account as a myth.

There have been many who have dismissed this hermit myth in the past, yet these are those same historians who, before the age of science and

GPR, declared that Master Wace was not a trustworthy recorder of history. We have seen how a lack of archaeological knowledge caused them to draw wrong conclusions.

Should there be permission granted by the church and English Heritage to examine the unmarked grave at Waltham Abbey, then we will have answers, but that is for later.

CHAPTER 5

After examining the truthfulness of the hermit story through the eyes of those skilled men and women who examine our most treasured and ancient documents, there are some who expressed their doubts as to the account in the Vita Haroldi being all myth. They include men like Walter De Grey Birch, British Anglo-Saxon academic, Talbot scholar, and translator of ancient manuscripts for the British museum, who, after spending many months translating the Vita Haroldi, said, 'Whether true or legendary we may never know.' Yet he confessed to feeling that there was a simple honesty about the manuscript. He noted Sir Thomas Duffus Hardy's report that there is some truth in the curious tale of Harold's survival. These scholars never allow themselves to swing out on a limb but go as far as they could without being controversial.

What to make of that comment made by the professor, 'there may be some truth in this curious document'? A lowering of his guard? A personal comment that reveals some private doubts he dare not fully commit to? How, when we examine for ourselves this document, are we to make sense of this comment? The Vita Haroldi is, in its entirety, a contradiction of the established recorded histories, so how can there be 'some truthfulness in this curious tale'?

The Norse Sagas

The Norse sagas are interesting because for some centuries, they were histories told as stories by storytellers who travelled from place to place, keeping their own histories alive. It was not until the twelfth century that these old tales were written down, and even though these stories may

43

have varied somewhat, the basic tales remained the same because these storytellers were early historians, interested in the survival of such tales and keeping the histories alive. Where our interest in these sagas lies has to do with the references to Harold.

The Hemings saga tells of Harold falling late in the battle and being found in the early morning before light, near death. He was taken and healed in Canterbury. Even though the location where Harold was healed in this saga maybe wrong, the choice of Canterbury might give us some clues as to where the source of the original information came from.

Like the other sagas, it speaks of what is known of Harold's movements up to the aftermath of the battle. He then tells the same story as all the other survival stories, but beyond those events immediately after the battle, it changes.

Could this be due to the jumble of information the writer was picking up from others long after the event? I find this interesting. Although the stories vary, they all begin the same: Harold was found in the early hours, was taken away, and was healed of his injuries.

Also, some of these stories, particularly the Norse sagas, were stories carried back to the Orkneys, and Scandinavia, after the battle as oral stories. Yet when we examine all the accounts from different sources, certain places and events that relate to the myth are repeated. There is a common thread. It begs the question, If there is no truth in these stories, why are there so many similarities?

National Geographic magazine spoke of ancient histories, and the sagas make a valid point. They point out, 'Historians in the 19th century accepted these accounts as mostly accurate accounts except where they venture into the mythology and fantasy, today they are viewed as partially romantic but still with historical relevance, so, still a crucial part of history.'

Are we sometimes guilty of missing the point of these sagas, throwing the baby out with the bathwater when discussing how accurate or inaccurate they are? Do we do these 'historians' an injustice by deriding the contents of these works as old wives' tales told by men?

It is assumed that because these stories were at times expanded upon, possibly to improve and heighten the excitement, then those parts of those tales that were true are lost.

Sverre Sigurdsson

This is borne out in the case of King Sverre Sigurdsson, who was the subject of a Norse saga and whose fantastic tales were for many years considered to be myth. His saga has confounded historians and archaeologists recently when events within the saga have been proven true.

The story was that in 1197, during a siege of his castle, he was eventually overcome, and the castle was burned. As a means of poisoning the water source, the 'Baglers' who were attacking threw one of his men down the well to poison the water. Then they threw stones down to prevent the people from being able to clean the well.

Archaeologist Anna Peterson, speaking from the dig in Trondheim, said, 'It's amazing, after all these years to realise what the saga told us was actually true!'

We have Snorri Sturluson, the great storyteller in the Norse tradition, a chieftain, lawyer, poet, and historian. These men were more than simple storytellers.

Below is the Icelandic saga in reference to Harold.

Jatvardar Saga

> After that King Harold made them set up his banner before him and went out to against William, and there was the greatest battle, and it seemed long uncertain which side would win the victory. But, as the fight went on, the loss of men turned on the English side, and a great host fell, and all fled who chose life. There fell king Harold and his brother Gurth, but Valtheof their brother fled out of the fight. William the bastard caused him to be burnt afterwards in a wood, and a hundred men with him. It is the story of Englishmen that in the night after the battle, some friends of king Harold fared to the battlefield and looked for his body, and found him alive, and bore him off to be healed; he was cured in secret. And when he was made whole, it was offered him by his friends to make war on William, and get the land whatever it cost. But

king Harold would not do that, stating he understood that God would not grant him the realm. And perhaps it is better so. Then the king took a better plan to give up this world's honour, and went into a cell and was a hermit while he lived, so serving Almighty God unceasingly both night and day.

The Hemings Pattr predates the Jatvardar saga by a century.

On the night after Harold Godwineson fell, an old cottager and his wife went to the battlefield to strip the bodies of the slain and get riches for themselves. They saw a great pile of bodies and noticed a bright light above it. They discussed it and said that there must be a holy man amongst the slain. They began to clear away the bodies where they had seen the light, and they saw the arm of a man sticking out of the heap of corpses. There was a large gold ring on it. The cottager took hold of the arm and asked whether the man was alive. He answered, 'I'm alive.'

The cottager said, 'Get the corpses off him—I think it's the king.'

They pulled the man up and asked if he could be healed. The king said, 'I think I could be healed, but I don't think you two could do it.'

The old woman said, 'We'll try.'

They picked him up, laid him in their cart, and went home with him. They kept him in secret and lied to King William's men when they come looking for Harold's body, following a trail of blood leading to their house. The old couple said that the woman had gone mad and killed their horse, and that was where the blood came from. (She acted mad to back up the story.) The king's men believed them and went back to tell William that Harold was dead and his body couldn't be found.

The validity and true origins of these histories matter. Most of us accept that although the events that changed history are true, the details that colour them—for us, the very character of those people involved in those events—are also important.

As an example of what I mean, imagine holding in our hands something from that time that was personal to that person, long dead. We don't say, 'Oh, this was from the twelfth century. Interesting.' Instead, we say, 'I wonder who this belonged to? What were they thinking all those years ago? I wonder if they had children? What did they look like?' We look long and hard at such items, and we desire to know as much as is possible about those people back then. We are not content with assumptions—we desire to know more. It is in us to enquire.

It is accepted that for written histories after the conquest, when it comes to how to spin the politics, the victors dictate the story. As we look back now, we can say much of what was written about Harold was based on propaganda written that way first, so it was accepted, right or wrong.

If a story has been quashed, we should try to find out why before we discard it. If you were a historian living in those times, would you fearlessly write what you believed to be the complete truth, or would you lean towards a politically correct rendition of events? Today we live in a democratic society where journalists can, and invariably do, say, 'Publish and be damned.' England back then was not that kind of place.

CHAPTER 6

These men who played major roles during the invasion—Harold, in the role of defender of England, and William, Duke of Normandy—are long gone. This is established history, and these events are beyond doubt. Harold was defeated, and Norman rule became law.

The Vita Haroldi

The document in its present form was copied from the scribe's own notes. These would have included earlier writings, kept safe in the church's archives, and would have included the works of those eminent canons who broke in opinion with the church fathers at the time regarding the question of the manner and events that surrounded Harold's death. This would have been a dispute of some significance at the time. The actual completed work of the Vita Haroldi, as is present in the British library, is said to have been written around a hundred or more years after the conflict in the late twelfth century, which means the original notes were earlier and the original parchment his notes were taken from were likely in need of copying, possibly because the condition after more than seventy years was poor.

This means it could have been written sometime around the reign of Henry II to the reign of King John. It was copied into the form it is now in at the British library from those earlier notes from canons or scribes.

The twelfth-century parchment those early notes were taken from was the original testimony of the last person to speak with Harold, his confessor, Andrew, a young monk at St John's Church, Chester. The Vita

Haroldi document was kept hidden at the church in Waltham for around four hundred years, carefully preserved by the fathers there.

What makes the Vita Haroldi of great importance historically is that it speaks of those days of the king after the Battle of Hastings, the most famous conflict in English history. It tells a story very different to the recorded history of the day.

As I have explained earlier, I had used the hermit myth in a series of three historical novels, and it had worked well in tying the thread together. The role of King Harold as a humble pilgrim travelling around Germany in the late eleventh century and meeting up with one of the heroes in the story fitted into the plot. Other writers had picked up on this myth and used it; writers like Rudyard Kipling had shown an interest in the compelling tale.

The Vita Haroldi tells the story of a Saracen woman who healed the badly wounded King Harold, who was close to death after he had been found on the battlefield by two local people. On the morning of 15 October 1066, after the battle had finished, they had been searching through the dead for some Saxons who may have still been alive. One asked who had said he was still in life, and Harold answered he was the king. He was under a body, and he still breathed. He was lifted out and taken in secret to Winchester, barely alive.

The Vita Haroldi tells us that after two years in the care of this woman, Harold eventually recovered and left England, travelling in secret to Europe in hope of raising an army. He eventually returned to England dressed as a pilgrim, called himself Christian, and died at an old age in Chester in 1112.

If we could just find evidence of such a woman ...

A Journey of Extraordinary Discovery

As with any historical research where little is known of a particular subject, it is a journey into the unknown. You must have hope that some new evidence may be discovered, and this hope empowers you. It was different for me because I had set out to prove this strange tale false.

When I began this particular search, I openly admitted that I hoped to find conclusive proof that the subject of my research, the Vita Haroldi, was exactly as it had been described by many historians, a myth. Upon uncovering this M/S Harley 3776, I remember being excited, because it was just what I had been looking for. so I was happy to accept it as an ancient myth.

But something about this story bothered me. Something I'd read during the initial research disturbed my peace. I needed to be able to put this document down, partly because I had what I needed for my novels and the information about the survival tale was no longer relevant to me, but also because I wanted to move on. However, the tormentor on my shoulder had other plans.

When I am making preparations for a new story which has invariably something to do with history, I try to research my stories thoroughly, so I concluded in respect of this ancient document that it was not my opinion that mattered. Having an opinion on a matter is far from the same as one knowing about a matter. I needed to roll up my sleeves, dive into the research, and put this myth to bed.

I was relatively uninformed on this myth, just a novelist with a passion for delving into history when a deeper understanding of a particular time was needed. What actually mattered to me was that I should get this right, find the truth, and seek out those who were informed on this particular chapter in our country's history why this story had been dismissed as a myth.

First, though, I focused on finishing my novels.

I used the story from the Vita Haroldi about the pilgrim Christian travelling around Europe within the three books I was writing. I went on to use what was my interpretation of the fictional, final discovery of the whereabouts of the old king of the English, Harold Godwin, buried in an unmarked grave at the east wall of his old abbey at Waltham. As a local, I know the secret that all those who live in the Abbey know. (The town is locally referred to as the Abbey.) This secret is that the stone marker in the Waltham Abbey's garden beyond the east wall that states, 'Here lies the body of Harold,' was opened in the late fifties and did not contain the body of King Harold, as is generally thought.

We have signs too, at each end of our town, stating, 'Waltham Abbey is the last resting place of King Harold, the last Saxon King of England.'

It is a minor consideration, but don't you have to have proof—in this case a body? I would suggest that the powers that be erect a suitable memorial, with the actual remains of King Harold buried beneath.

I contacted professors of Saxon history and spoke with them; one was a lecturer from Chester

I was given reference works to look over, and he told me that he would raise the subject with some of his colleagues and get back to me. This was very kind, and I appreciated his efforts.

When he got back to me, he explained that the general consensus of opinion amongst his colleagues was that the story was a myth. I thanked him and asked if he had looked into the myth personally, and he admitted that he had not. I admit that I was hoping for a little more than a consensus of opinion. Hopes of an early resolution faded, and I felt resolved to roll up my sleeves again and continue researching the subject myself.

I joined the local historical society, the Waltham Abbey Historical Society (WAHS). At the time, the group was headed up by an eminent archaeologist, Peter Huggins. I found the group quite cordial, very knowledgeable on certain subjects, and all pretty certain that the story from the Vita Haroldi was a myth.

'Excellent!' I thought. 'Someone will certainly be able to direct me to the relevant research tools to further inform me.' At the time, I was of the same mind and felt it was a myth, even though at this juncture, I had not delved into the subject in any great depth.

I decided that in order to connect the dots in a search like this, it was about looking back and gaining perspective. This is where we begin. I hoped to look at the personal losses and gains of those involved. It was to be an examination of, and for me a unique peek at, the personal journey of our last Saxon king, and, after 960 years, the possible secrets that he and his close and loyal friends and family kept.

A Chance Conversation That Changed My Thinking

I remember very clearly my chat with Peter Huggins, the local archaeologist. I remember because his response to my question set a small fire in me. I asked him if he believed the myth. He replied, 'No, and there is no evidence! The remains of the king, brought back to Waltham by either Edith, Harold's wife, or Gytha, his mother, have been moved up to three times due to building works. The last known place it was seen was in the cellar of the rectory, so it is just not true he is buried in Chester.'

(This referred to St John's, where the Vita Haroldi states he died and was originally buried.)

I must admit to feeling taken aback by the abruptness of his response. It was as if he'd been asked this question many times before and had no desire to elucidate. I asked him if he had noticed the strange mason's marks in the old east wall. These were in the form of arrows approximately three metres apart and indicating a symbol in the centre, much like a crown. I had looked closely at all the stonework around the abbey as research for my novels, hoping to find something, some strange configuration within the actual stonework, that would lend some feeling of authenticity to my work, and I had discovered these marks. These marks suited my plans because they were subtle enough without being obvious. I imagined readers of the trilogy searching the walls around the church after being drawn into my story—a storyteller's dream, I suppose.

Yet even though I still considered the alternative Harold's story to be a myth at the time, my tummy told me something just did not add up. Then, my views about this story of Harold escaping changed in a moment, and unbeknownst to Peter, it was what he said next that was to profoundly affect my view on this most controversial of subjects. In fact, it was pivotal in my journey, in my gaining more understanding of this most interesting case.

'This section,' he said, indicating the old section of wall that contained the mason's marks, 'was built around AD 1100. The stones are just random stones they used to build this section. I don't believe they are significant.'

I can still clearly remember that moment, because his words caused me to change the way I had been approaching this research. I had fallen into a common trap that of trying the easy route, asking someone who is deemed learned instead of rolling up my sleeves and doing my own digging.

I remembered something I had read while researching the Vita Haroldi document, and those little titbits of information had stored away in my head somewhere. And so it was that those seemingly unconnected pieces of an unfathomable conundrum began to form a definable shape inside my head. Suddenly it began to make sense.

If Harold had survived the battle and had actually ended up dying in Chester many years later, what time period are we talking about? Around 1100? I did not know at the time what I know now, yet still the dating was significant. If this section of the old church east wall was built around the early 1100s, then the mason's marks could be important!

CHAPTER 7

I am a stone mason, and it has taught me to recognise certain marks left by other masons, whether last week or nine hundred years ago.

Peter Huggins was giving his opinion, and I understood that, but his area of expertise was not in the constructing of stone buildings but the examination of ancient artefacts. Peter, without realising it at the time, had stepped out of his sphere of experience and made a judgement on my area of experience, stonework.

I knew those marks were significant, that they were not just random lumps of stone but were trying to tell us all something. In fact, for nine hundred years they had been trying to tell of their secret.

Many times during my years of building stone structures, I would leave marks cut into the stone for a variety of reasons. In the following pages, I have shown the section of wall in question. The symbols I refer to can be seen at each side and central; I have exaggerated them slightly with black ink.

Two darts on each side point to the middle and a curious shaped stone like a bowtie. The central symbol is the marker.

By the end of my conversation with Peter that afternoon, I had to rethink my approach to this research. I remembered my studies on the changes in meaning in some areas of the ancient Greek language. *Mythos* was a word used to describe a story whose origins were rooted in truthfulness. It's where we get the term *myth*.

An historical paradox!

Three seemingly unconnected pieces of information I remembered at that time popped into my head and raised the initial doubt that drove me on. Three points of reference from my brief, almost disinterested preamble into the dubious credibility of this curious book, are seen as important enough to have hidden throughout four hundred years of the abbey's life.

1. The stonemason's marks. Why would a stonemason go to the trouble of leaving markers that would survive centuries past his time?

59

2. The random comment from Master Wace. Why did the chronicler of the Master Wace histories of the Norman conquest state (seemingly cryptically) that the body of Harold was in the choir of his church (Harold's old church)?

3. The date of the east wall construction. If, as has been suggested, Harold was brought back from Chester to be buried at his own church, when would that have been? Early in the twelfth century?

The section of wall dated by Professor Peter Huggins as early twelfth century. I have indicated mark I identified as significant in yellow pen.

Family Concerns and the Sad Death of My Wife

Following the meeting with Peter Huggins, my wife and I took a holiday in Corfu. It occurred to Julie on the flight back to Stanstead Airport that our frequent breaks away made us a higher risk of accidental death, and we agreed that should an accident befall us, it would likely be both of us who would die together. With five children, our concerns were that they should not be burdened with the cost of a double funeral, and so on our return, I arranged a life policy for both of us. Two weeks later, Julie, my wife of forty-one years, was diagnosed with pancreatic cancer, and the focus of myself and my family was on Julie and her treatment. This was in July 2011.

During the chemotherapy sessions at UCLH Euston, London, we discussed her care together. We agreed our youngest daughter, Lauren, was best placed to take on the major part of her care because I had to continue to work.

We had all focused so hard on finding a cure that when Julie came to the end of her fight, it caught us all out. A good friend of mine and Julie's, Caroline Kwouk, took me to one side and, seeing the hope we as a family had that somehow it would be OK, whispered to me, 'Peter? Prepare yourself. Julie is not going to beat this.' It was the first moment I had to face us continuing without her.

The morning before the afternoon she died, I was tidying up a small job a mile from the house when Lauren phoned me. Lauren had always been strong, and she had coped with this situation as one who was more mature than her twenty-nine years, but I will always remember this short conversation.

'Dad? I don't know what to do. I can't stop this. Can you come, please?'

I dropped my tools and drove home, and as I turned up towards our home at Waltham Abbey, there was a cue of traffic all the way to the town. Someone from the council had decided to re-tarmac a three-foot section of path outside MacDonald's and had set up a four-way traffic light system. It took an hour to travel three hundred metres, and on that day of all days.

Lauren had called the nurse, and they had administered the morphine and left as I got there. I sat with her and held her as she slipped away.

She died on a dark, grey, miserable afternoon on 23 November 2012. I have never felt so low. A profound sense of helplessness reduced me by sucking the life out of me. I was the husband, the father of five grown adults, the provider and solver of all problems. It was my job to care for those I love, and I could not fight this. I felt helpless and useless.

The life insurance was a problem. They refused to pay out due to Julie visiting our family doctor three times during the week before her diagnosis. She was told she had IBS and was given laxatives. I appealed. The appeal failed because it was explained that should her visits to the doctor have been reported at the time, then Ageas would have postponed the policy until Julie felt better.

I had to return to work. It was to be many months before I could begin to function again. I tried to pick up where I left off in my search for Harold but was dealing with my own health problems. Bouts of sepsis rendered me incapacitated for two hours at a time with shaking fits where I could not stand or see clearly. The only thing that worked was for me to run a very hot bath and lie as low as I could, until slowly the shaking stopped. Swollen belly, vomiting, many trips to emergency in ambulance or car—all this was exacerbated by the loss of Julie.

I was diagnosed with Crohn's disease, and it was to be some

twenty-three months of treatment and operations before I was strong enough to continue my search.

14 October 2014
Waltham Abbey
The Scan

After some time, I returned to work and again gave thought to the Vita Haroldi. I was convinced the symbols in the east wall were directions from a bygone age, and I arranged for a ground-penetrating radar (GPR) scan through the good offices of Sumo Archaeological Services. This was the company that had assisted in the search for the remains of Richard III in Leicester.

After securing a permit for a nonintrusive search of the grounds east of the east wall, I paid the two-thousand-pound fee, and the scan was carried out. It attracted quite a lot of media attention at the time, and although I was advised by local and national historians that it would resolve nothing, I was determined to find out.

The criticism from these knowledgeable sources was perfectly justified on the face of it. After all, I was looking for a body in a plot to the rear of an old church that had stone markers. In other words, it was a graveyard!

One historian, John Hill, who had been heavily involved with the search for Richard III and who was interviewed with me on a local BBC radio program, was sceptical but agreed that what I was trying to do—find the remains of our last Saxon king—was still worth pursuing.

In my view, it was not a waste of time, and John proved to be the voice of reason amongst so many other voices at that time. He gave me just

The East Wall
Waltham Abbey

Above is the section of early twelfth-century
wall with the masons markings

enough encouragement to help me pursue my goal. However, had he and the whole world been dismissive of my research, I would still have arranged the scan because I felt sure the stone markers were accurate.

The Unmarked Grave

The day of the scan, the east wall was like a film set. We had Peter Huggins, the local archaeologist; the national and local papers; a film crew who are friends of mine, from Scope TV productions; many locals who came to give support; and the team of archaeologists from the survey team.

During the survey, the archaeologists who were carrying out the scan kept quietly indicating to me that they had definitely found something of interest in an open area of grass. I was convinced that the body would be closer to the east wall and asked if they could make sure that section could be well scanned, which they did. However, they were excitedly referring me back to the open patch of grass. It was to be some weeks before I realised that what they had found, and were indicating to me excitedly during the search, was what I was looking for. What they had found was so crucial to the search.

I had a nervous two-week wait for the results. The important sheet, the results of the scan, are below. See if you can spot what I missed at first. When I realised what I was looking at, it was quite a moment.

The unmarked grave is in the centre, marked as red. I examined closely the plan of church three, as illustrated in archaeologist Peter Huggins's paper, entitled 'The Church at Waltham: An Archaeological and Historical Review'.

I placed the survey findings, showing the position of the unmarked grave, over Peter's plan of church three, Harold's old church, and the findings show the unmarked grave is exactly where the Master Wace continuator described, central to the choir and directly behind the old altar.

On looking at the findings of our scan, it shows clearly that when

Placing the plan of Harold's church over location of the unmarked grave shown below, places the unmarked grave in the exact position, as described by Master Wace.

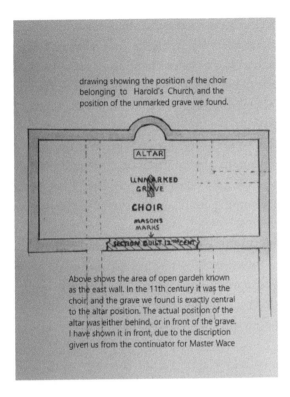

drawing showing the position of the choir belonging to Harold's Church, and the position of the unmarked grave we found.

ALTAR

UNMARKED GRAVE

CHOIR

MASONS MARKS

SECTION BUILT 12TH CENT.

Above shows the area of open garden known as the east wall. In the 11th century it was the choir, and the grave we found is exactly central to the altar position. The actual position of the altar was either behind, or in front of the grave. I have shown it in front, due to the discription given us from the continuator for Master Wace

Note:

There are no other un-marked graves showing up on the scans, in this area. This is important as one of the arguments made by historians was that, as this is land attached to the church, there are bound to be many graves. The archaeological team found 'marker stones', on the surface, but just the one 'un-marked grave' we found.

Master Wace spoke cryptically of the actual place where Harold was buried, he said,

> He that wishes to know this,
> at Waltham, behind the high altar
> can find this self-same altar,
> and Harold, lying in the choir.

I believe the continuator for Master Wace was speaking about Harold's church—church three, not, as was originally thought,---church four.

As the scan clearly shows, the placing of this grave is accurate to within an inch central, in direct line with the wall markings. The wall has been dated by our archaeologist, Peter Huggins, as being built some time from early 1100s during the building of church four. I believe that because the completion of church four was not until around the 1150's, this places both the internment of Harold (should this indeed be his grave) and the curious stonemason's marks, being secretly completed at the same time.

This was when the penny dropped, and we realised what we had discovered. I used the page taken from the work 'The Church at Waltham', by P. Huggins. My initial calculations were taken from the walls uncovered by the GPR.

I have shown all the relevant points of reference and shown the shaded walls of church three from Peter Huggins's studies.

The previous pages show the position of the 'unmarked' grave that was found to be directly in line with the central mason's mark in the east wall.

The plan I sketched shows the old church foundations found by Peter Huggins.

I have drawn this diagram from the GPR scans and measured to precise distances between the old foundations, and the centre location where the dean's seat would have been marked the position of the altar as indicated by Peter Huggins, our archaeologist. I then lined up the centre marks made by the twelfth-century mason, cut into the twelfth-century wall, with the position of the unmarked grave we discovered. You can see in the earlier diagram.

What I found exciting was the actual position of the unmarked grave. As you can see, in the diagram I've drawn of the scanned area at the east wall, the unmarked grave was exactly central to the choir and in line with where the altar was positioned. I measured the distance off the original scan sheet, and the actual distance from the centre of the position of the grave to the walls of the old church on both sides was to within an inch central. When this body was interned sometime during the twelfth century, it is clear that great care was taken to make sure it was in exactly the correct position.

Something else surprised me—something that surprised many of the historians who thought the scanning of the east wall was pointless, because of the likelihood of finding many graves. In actual fact, there were not 'many graves'. It's true that the position of the unmarked grave disappointed me initially, because I had been convinced the area it needed to be was close to the mason's marks in the east wall. Then I reviewed again the description of Master Wace. I apologise for repeating what I've said before, but this amazing discovery took us by surprise, and it took some looking over before we fully accepted our own findings, so allow me to recap.

> He that wishes to know this
> at Waltham, behind the high altar,
> can find this self-same altar,
> and King Harold lying in the choir.

We know that in the early 1100s, the Norman church was under construction, so it seems logical to assume that the altar that belonged to the old church, Harold's church, would still be in use for some time, because it was actually much later in that century when the new church was completed. I would assume that the altar and choir would have still been located in Harold's old church. This would make sense, and looking at the position of the unmarked grave, it is central to the choir and behind the old altar position where the altar was originally, in Harold's church.

I returned to the east wall to measure again, to be sure that the position of the unmarked grave in comparison to the choir walls that had been mapped out and marked by Professor Peter Huggins. The position of the unmarked grave is, to within an inch, central to those walls.

Could this be the unmarked grave of King Harold?

Other Factors to Consider

The church's historical records, which for centuries have been under the entitlement of 'official', state that the body Edith brought back was moved three times because of new building work.

The very fact that the body we have discovered has clearly not moved position since this time could mean it's not the body moved three times for building work. But if, as has been suggested, the body was moved three times, but each time it was replaced in exactly the same place, then this too is exciting, because it could mean that should an excavation be allowed, then many of the questions concerning the manner of Harold's death can be resolved.

Excited by this discovery, a friend and fresh convert from the historical society, Clive, and I took this new evidence to the area head of English Heritage. Joining us was the vicar and the council representative for Waltham Abbey antiquities. As we entered the church, it was quite clear from the expressions on their faces that the meeting would not go well—no welcoming smiles, no handshakes. It seemed that what concerned them the most was the amount of press interest this discovery had aroused. There had been reporters calling at the vicarage and upsetting the vicar. The representative of English Heritage had been contacted at her office in Cambridge, and she was not happy. I was told that the grave, although showing as unmarked, had been undisturbed for so long that there was no reason to disturb it. I could see her point, yet this was our last Saxon king we were talking about.

I offered that it was in the national interest because when a king of such high prominence was discovered, it was only right and decent that he be honoured with a suitable marker. She replied, 'We do not dig up bodies just to satisfy your curiosity.' I felt like a Prometheus who had stolen fire from the gods of English Heritage, or that I had opened up Pandora's box, except this time even hope was lost.

I wonder if anyone tried to squash Lord Carnarvon when Howard Carter found King Tut.

We tried to explain why we were so sure the grave was likely that of King Harold, and they agreed. 'Yes, it is very likely that, after looking at the scan results, it is Harold in the unmarked grave.' But she would not agree to an actual dig.

Then, as if hammering in a final nail, the vicar, in a flamboyant sweeping gesture with arms waving and all the fearsome incandescence of a scorned mistress, declared, 'I will do all in my power to ensure this exhumation will never take place.' And that was the moment when the hope of so many of the locals of Waltham Abbey was unceremoniously cut off.

It is widely known that the present grave so many visit every year does not hold the remains of King Harold, so it is a sham. These honest locals would love for visitors to visit the actual burial place of our last Saxon king and know for certain that it is not a shameful sham of an empty grave but the true, last resting place of King Harold II.

We were quite taken aback, especially because not six months before, the same vicar and I had chatted at the east wall, and he had declared his great excitement at hearing of my searching for Harold.

It seems we were ganged up on, bushwhacked by English Heritage and the church.

I find it short-sighted and hypocritical that thirteenth-century graves of monks at Westminster Abbey are opened up and examined with the approval of these same bodies, the church and English Heritage, and that for the progress and expansion of our railway, thousands of 'correctly buried' souls, safely interred in formally consecrated ground, can be dug up at St Pancras, London; examined in a laboratory; and replanted somewhere else—all with the blessing of English Heritage and the church. Yet one unloved and falsely maligned lost king is left in an obscure, unmarked, and forgotten grave.

Of course, this setback in no way dampened my enthusiasm, and I was all the more determined to find out the truth of the myth, but it was at this time my Crohn's disease worsened. I was hospitalised and spent the next two years in and out of hospital, culminating in an emergency operation in which two feet of large bowel and part of my small intestines were removed. I then spent seven months with a stoma bag attached to my stomach.

A close friend of mine, Annie Sabbagh, helped get me through those dark days. She was and will always remain a good friend. It was through Annie that I met Tim Jones and David Hatter, TV producers whose company was recording and following my journey. Annie was a former head nurse at Great Ormond Street Hospital. She helped me through the nightmare of treatments and bag changes, asking the right questions when doctors did their rounds, making sure I ate the right mixtures, and providing quantities of cooked foods. I am forever in her debt.

After the removal of the stoma bag, I spent some months resting. Then in 2016, I decided I needed to continue with the search for answers.

CHAPTER 8

In 2016, I was free at last of the stoma bag, and although I was greatly reduced in weight, I felt stronger and in better health than I had for some years.

Almost five years after the death of Julie, I married again, to an old friend of my wife's, and we joined in this search together. Frances had become my researcher during those days we had searched around Shropshire, and we became good friends first. Gradually it developed into a closer relationship, which was of great benefit to me because her understanding of history is invaluable.

As it happens, my change of circumstance was much to the relief of my youngest daughter, Lauren Simone, who after bravely and very loyally caring full-time for Julie, turned her attention to me.

I realise this is not pertinent to the search, yet I am bound to mention from time to time those around me who empowered and enabled me during those tumultuous times.

I look back and realise our respective roles of father-protector, and daughter-dependant changed because for a time I became preoccupied with trying to put back together or repair something that could not be mended, and those events eventually caused me to accept that nothing in our lives is forever and that a particular chapter of my life had irretrievably broken.

After years of raising children and the toll that takes on you, Julie and I had happily arrived at pension age and that most edifying time of the rediscovery of our forgotten freedom. We were enjoying more frequent breaks, holidays in the Greek Isles, and weekends in York and Bath. Sadly these were cut short so quickly, and with barely the time to face that horror and say our goodbyes.

During those dark days just after Julie's death, I would continually discover Lauren 'in my pocket', metaphorically speaking. There were phone calls at 2 a.m. asking me in accusatory tones reminiscent of my mother, 'Where are you?' She worried she would find me incapacitated somewhere while I was still in the grip of some reckless excess. I remember believing that the terrible sense of loss was to be the end of me, yet those concerns of my children drew me back so many times.

I had the great fortune at this time to meet a former nurse, Annie, whom I have already mentioned. We shared a common interest, in that both of us had lost our soulmates.

It was Annie, with her matronal air and clippity shoes, who would march through the wards and advise and enquire during my long illness when dealing with doctors and nurses. She was a powerful mixture of fearsome and kind. I remain forever in her debt.

As is true with most painful episodes in our lives, those dark days eventually run their course; although they never leave you, they allow you to continue. And so I began the process of refocussing. My new wife, Frances, is both beautiful and intelligent, but I have discovered this: she thinks like a man. She has an aptitude for seeing around corners, looking at evidence, and deciphering the data in a three-dimensional way. Her experiences in the field of research, having worked for many years for the British Government—very hush-hush—has helped us move on at a pace with our searches as she takes the approach of an investigator poring over a crime scene.

After the scan at the east wall, Frances and I found ourselves agreeing on the question of the myth. We began to openly discuss the possible validity of the alternative story. Many times our gut feelings would take us in different directions, and we would beaver away, researching on our own. Yet we still compared notes and finds because we had to work together if we were to find answers.

Quick Review

After looking over the results of our findings, we have an unmarked grave!

I believe it to be the final resting place of King Harold.

Certainly the evidence points to this spot at the east wall.

If Harold survived the battle in 1066 and later died in Chester, could it be possible that at some point after he'd died, the monks in Chester and the monks in Waltham agreed Harold's remains should be returned to his own church?

If this was done in the early years of the twelfth century, possibility the 1120s, and if this was the body of Harold as referred to in the work of Master Wace, whose writings were composed around 1160, then there is a case for optimism (or making an educated guess) that this could be the body of the old hermit. But we'll put that on the back burner for now, because there is a way to go in this search for answers.

An Important Script in Ancient Latin

While reading through many ancient documents, I came across a section of fourteenth-century Latin script that made a reference to a meeting in 1125 at Woodstock, which was at the time the new home of King Henry I. I am fortunate that the friends I have made over the years are varied in their chosen professions. One has been most helpful, a friend who is a Latin professor, James Lacy. I asked him to translate the script into English, making notes on any nuances he may pick up on to give a clearer insight into the true message in the document. What follows is the translation.

Chronica Monasterii De Melsa

Gurtha, who advised Harold to withdraw from that same war, confirmed, in the presence of King Henry I at Wodestoke in the 25th year of his reign, dressed as a hermit, with a lorica over his bare skin, that the said Harold had escaped from the battle alive, and was recently buried, not at Waltham, but in Chester. For the aforesaid—Henry— seriously wounded, escaped the payment of death, with the benefit of the night. Having been cared for, however, with his mind weighed down by the enormity of his crime, because this had resulted in not only the destruction of one man or of one state, but in the blood of countless people, and in the loss of freedom of all his nation, and the eternal destruction of his kingdom, he turned totally to lamentation, and totally to repentance; he committed himself completely to divine piety, exchanging his royal insignia for a dark-grey garment, and he put on the garb of a penitent and first appeared openly in the cave of a certain rock near Canterbury, in which he lived as a hermit, performing several purification sacrifices. But, since his fame was starting to spread, a considerable number of people, from both far and near, began spending time with him, to such an extent, that he strove to take away any memory of himself among them. Afterwards, indeed, it was understood that he lived for many years, as a hermit, not far from Chester.

And at that same place, in the time of Henry I, in the 12th year of his reign, he, at the point of death, finally confessed who he was, to a priest who was aware of his secrets. And so, tired out by a long old age, and dying, full of days, he went the way of all mortals. He was buried at Chester in the Church of St John the Confessor, behind the altar, before the altar of St Nicholas some 46 years after the Conquest.

Reading through the context, the 'Henry' mentioned should be read as Harold.

When Frances and I looked over this piece, the footnote, added by an eighteenth-century historian, says to the effect, 'It is likely not true.' We found, though, that there were sufficient places and references mentioned that needed to be examined and researched before we could accept an eighteenth-century presumption.

References to Research

What follows were the clues we looked over. At first it appeared that there was not a lot to go on, particularly because we are talking about a time when little by way of written works of that time is available to scrutinise now. So problem number one, the Saxons were not known for being 'concerned' with recording their histories, and two, it had been nine hundred years!

As for the eighteenth-century historian whose conclusion was that this was 'likely' not true, we disagreed with him. But how were we to set about proving this document as true? We had to go to Canterbury.

What hope did Frances and I set out with? Not much, I have to admit. Did we believe we would travel to Canterbury and find some amazing proof after all those years that Harold had survived—oh, and that his survival was a well-kept secret?

In truth, it was a leap of faith.

The trip was a day out, and we liked Canterbury. Our expectations were not high, and we were resolved to enjoy the day. We did look over what information we had as we drove south. These clues were drawn from a very brief conversation that was written nine hundred years ago, translated from Latin, and recorded by someone who thought it to have enough historical significance to warrant mentioning it. We broke it down into the following.

'Having been cared for'
'Turning to lamentation'
'Committed to divine piety'
'Wearing the garb of a penitent'
'In the cave of a certain rock' (Reference: Canterbury)
'Living as a Hermit'
'Carrying out several purification sacrifices'

We were already planning our next trip as we drove down to Canterbury: Chester. Another part of the conversation between King Henry I and Gurth was that Harold had 'lived as a hermit, not far from Chester'.

This next translation is the original translated text. As you will see as you read through both translations, the professor's translation had picked out the meanings from the nuances within the original text. I found that reading both gave up more information, hidden within the ancient Latin.

First Translation from Original Latin

Gurth, who gave advice to Harold when he had withdrawn himself from that very same war, in the presence of King Henry I at Wodestoke in the 25th year of his reign, clothed in a cuirass on the nude skin in the way of a hermit, confirmed the report that Harold had escaped the battle alive and was recently buried not near Waltham but at Cestria. Aforesaid Henry had namely heavily wounded escaped the payment of death under the benefit of the night.

His mind was freed from the enormity of his crime, because it was not in the destruction of a single man or of a single town, but in the blood of countless people and in the loss of the freedom, libertatis ruina, of his people and in the eternal destruction of his kingdom.

He committed to divine piety, changing his royal insignia for a grey garment and taking the garment of repentance. He first openly appeared in the cave of some 'cujusdam' [a certain rock'] rock near Dorobernia [Canterbury], in which he lived as a hermit, performing some purificatory sacrifices. But, because as his fame was spreading, not a small multitude of people [popularis frequentia] both of living far away and nearby [came] to him, it happened that it was discovered by some people who he was, he tried [satagebat] to take away the memory of him amongst us.

Afterwards however it was understood that he had for a long time lived as a hermit during many years not far from Cestria [Chester].

At that moment, in the time of the foresaid King
Henry I, in the twelfth year of his reign, he, under great
pressure (positus in extremis), confessed finally to a priest
who he was, in order that the priest would be conscious
of his secrets.

And so, tired by a long old age and having fulfilled his
days, he died and went the way of mortals. He was buried
at Cestria in the Church of Saint John the Confessor,
behind the [main?] altar before the altar of Saint Nicolas.
So he had lived after the conquest some 46 years.

This testimony, which relates for us a conversation that took place in
1125, recopied in 1390, was dismissed by the eighteenth-century historian
as 'likely untrue'. Let's look for a moment at what was reported to have
been the nub of the content.

King Henry I had just built his new estate in Woodstock and had
imported animals from different parts of the world. He invited guests from
across England to a gathering, and amongst these were esteemed members
of the church. He also invited a guest of special interest, a former member
of the English royal family, Gurth of the Godwins. He wanted to know
if the rumours of King Harold escaping the battlefield in 1066 were true.

He was told that they were true, and that Harold had lived a long life
and had died in Chester. This is not what has been recorded in our histories
from the eleventh century onward. On finding this recorded in the ancient
Latin document, the historian decided it could not be a truthful account
and dismissed it.

CHAPTER 9

Gurth

At this point, I want to refer back to the battle and the section that covers the falling of both Harold and Gurth. This new evidence changes history as it has been recorded for nine hundred years. Established history has always insisted that Gurth died alongside Harold and Leofwine in 1066. This is an assumption, and this makes the Latin document we uncovered quite relevant—and very exciting.

It could be a confirmation that although Master Wace records that Gurth fell while attempting to reach Harold, he survived and possibly was one of those who, after dark, helped rescue his brother.

We know Leofwine was on the battlefield because of the mention of his being in charge of the Fyrdmen on Harold's right flank. We must assume that he died that day, because we have found no evidence or mention of his surviving.

After examining this new document and comparing it with the Vita Haroldi, it was interesting to note that the versions had similarities, but with this latest document, there was a little more information.

Upon reading through both accounts, it seems likely that this 'meeting' between Henry I and Gurth, Harold's younger brother, was reported on from different sources. I believe this was a social event where certain dignitaries of both church and state were invited.

Certainly the meeting was recorded by the compilers of church history, and later as recorded, this same information was added to the works of the Monesterii De Melsa but also likely by Martin, Abbot of Waltham.

With our thinking caps firmly on, we began to reason on all the information before us. If this recorded conversation between Henry I and

Gurth was a lie, what purpose would that have served? There was little to gain
or lose by entering this lie into the Monesterii De Melsa, a truthful registry of
all matters pertaining to the church of the time, and written by devout scribes.

Again we sought answers to those same questions.

Why did Master Wace cryptically add to his histories this quote: 'He
that wishes to know this, at Waltham, behind the high altar, can find this
self-same altar, and King Harold lying in the Choir'?

If Harold had been buried behind the altar at St John's, Chester, in
1112, and this was now 1124, would Abbot Martin not ask Abbot Andrew
at Chester to return their (Waltham Abbey's) patron?

Master Wace wrote his chronicles towards the end of the 1100s, and the
Woodstock meeting was 1124. Sometime between, isn't it reasonable to believe
that Harold could have been returned to his own church, where the monks
who adored him could rest, knowing their patron now truly rested in a position
befitting their king? They would no longer have to suffer the pretence if it was
known that the body Edith brought back was not that of King Harold.

The logical next move was to travel to Canterbury armed with this new
information, a boatload of faith, and absolutely no idea where to even begin
looking. It was a bright, sunny Sunday morning when Frances and I set off
from our home in Waltham Abbey, bound for Canterbury.

As we drove, we went over the pertinent passages in the text. 'A cave!'
'A certain rock!' 'Purificatory sacrifices!'

'These could mean anything,' I said. I still remember thinking that
the obvious place to look for caves would be along the banks of the River
Stour, somewhere between the coast and Canterbury.

Being realistic, we had to face the obvious question. What could we
possibly discover that would move our search forward? A cave with some
message cut into the limestone? I realised that the most likely outcome to
this trip was a complete blank. The odds were against us, I knew, yet still
we drove on.

When we arrived in Canterbury, we parked by the railway station and
walked towards the east gate. We decided to walk along the Stour, the old
river that passed by the city. It was a glorious spring morning, a Sunday, with
many families and tourists taking the air and enjoying the riverbank walk.

The reference to 'sacrificial cleansing' could, we thought, mean
freshwater, yet would we find a cave from nine hundred years ago? As

we walked, we discussed the problem of the passing of time. We had to consider the position of the River Stour now, and nine hundred years ago. We realised this was a problem. Rivers don't stay constant; their routes change. Frances saying out loud this obvious consideration made my shoulders sag and my optimism fade.

Another negative was that the land around Canterbury was flat! There were no rising banks where one would chance upon a cave cut out of the limestone; there were just flat grasslands. We saw no high ground that could be interpreted as 'a certain rock'.

'We could spend a week looking for something that may not even exist after so long,' I pointed out.

And yet here we were, out together, enjoying the day on a beautiful afternoon while on a peaceful riverside walk! I was still pleased we had made the effort. I believe that as keen as we were to find something tangible to help our research, we both had begun to just enjoy the day.

I looked across to my left as a punt silently glided past us, heading back towards the cafe where the tourists booked their boat rides. There was an older English chap explaining historical events to the passengers as he lowered the punt pole and leaned on it, pushing the punt on. A young Japanese couple chatted excitedly in their mother tongue, and the young girl, being the most vocal, translated for her boyfriend the histories of Canterbury. The melodic timbre of her voice, was incongruous yet pleasant in those very English of surroundings.

I remember thinking this oldish chap with the full, thick, dark brown beard was not the normal punt aficionado. Most tended to be young students of history who earned extra pocket money from taking out the tourists on their breaks from studying. I remember pointing him out to Frances as a bit of fun and saying, 'He looks like a professor of sorts. I wonder if he would have any ideas about this "certain rock", or the purification sacrifices!'

It occurred to us as we chatted that if these were purification sacrifices that Harold had been administering, it might involve a freshwater spring. I thought no more about it as we walked on.

Later, as we strolled back into the city, we drew level with the little cafe where the tourists hired a boat and a guide, and we decided to stop for a coffee. As we sipped our coffee and watched the comings and goings, Frances prompted me to ask at the bar about the reason for our trip.

The young chap I spoke to was from New Zealand and knew nothing about the history. I asked the older woman who ran the cafe, and she too knew little of its history, but as she spoke, she indicated to a chap behind me. He had just finished taking an old Japanese couple on a trip. 'He will know something. He's my husband, and he is a history professor!'

I turned around, and the oldish chap I'd seen earlier with the thick, full beard stood behind me.

'Ah!' I exclaimed. 'I saw you earlier, on the punt!'

He nodded. 'Yes, I help out once in a while. How can I help?'

I asked him if he knew of any 'springs' or places where they would have carried out purification sacrifices back in the eleventh century. I have to explain that at this point in our day, Frances and I had come to accept that the day had become just a pleasant jaunt. Even as I spoke to this chap, I could hear the tired hopelessness in my tone, and I was already hearing his particular rationale on the problems of time and relevant study material on obscure topics, and so resigned myself I waited for his response.

I was surprised to observe him thinking. After a momentary pause, as he thought over my question, he said this.

> 'There were two places around Canterbury where they used springwater. One was beyond the cathedral, but later the monks piped it in for the cathedral's private use. The other one was at Harbledown, about a mile out of town. This I would say is the most likely. Here is where the pilgrims who walked the pilgrim road would stop for the night and wash to cleanse themselves.
>
> Then, walking up to the top of the hill in the morning, cleansed and purified, they would look down on the city and the cathedral, spread out before them, before continuing on to Canterbury. Behind the spring, there was originally a cave, but this was walled up in the time of the Black Prince. It is now known as the well of the Black Prince.

Excited by this news, we thanked him and set off for this small hamlet just a mile outside of Canterbury.

Harbledown

The illustration on the following page is an artist's impression of the Black Prince well, formally the spring used by pilgrims in Saxon times on their way to Canterbury. Back in Saxon times, it was a low cave, worn away over the centuries by the constant flow of water from the spring. We don't know the depth of the cave because the wall face now obscures it.

I want to reiterate what the history professor told us. The Black Prince was Edward, prince of Wales, who was the eldest son of Edward III. If this is where Harold carried out acts of purification, on whom did he perform these?

This is where it gets interesting. As we researched this place, we discovered that one of the items uncovered around the well was a leather bucket, used to gather water in ancient times. Also, there was a cave here before it was walled up in the fourteenth century, where cleansing sacrifices were performed for the travel-weary pilgrims.

The old Roman road Watling Street runs right through this small town. It was a very busy road in the former days with Pilgrims and holy men. 'This could be the place,' I said.

'Cleansing sacrifices?' Frances agreed, and it was as we stood together, quietly collecting our thoughts before the old well, that we agreed we needed to research the history of this place much more thoroughly.

What we found excited us, and we were beginning to realise that this was more than a convenient watering hole for pilgrims back in the Middle Ages. This place was special.

As we uncovered these particular histories, I needed to remind myself that there was a distinct danger we might read into our discoveries more than was there and fall into the trap of offering suppositions as probables. All we could do was present the evidence as we found it.

Harbaldown

If this place was to hold answers to our questions, there had to be more to this place than a spring! While looking back over the description given us from the AD 1390 reference in the *Chronica Monasterii de Melsa*, we

75

ran through those recorded words of Gurth. 'He first openly appeared in the cave of a certain rock near Dorobernia in which he lived as a hermit, performing some purificatory sacrifices.'

We may have found the cave by arriving in Canterbury that morning with virtually no hope of finding even a smidgeon of evidence. We had found a cave! But we knew that this was not enough. We needed more— much more—if we were to establish any credibility to the ancient Latin document we had found.

Even so, after that first visit to Harbledown, we left feeling very excited. After all, we had expected to find nothing of great note that first time. We returned home feeling we had more than exceeded our expectations in discovering the well, and with good reason. It seemed likely we had found the possible location described in the Latin manuscript, the manuscript Professor James Lacy had deciphered for us. It spoke of a place where 'sacrifices of cleansing' were carried out. It was one of only two springs used in the time of the Norman conquest, and the other seemed to be primarily for the monks at the cathedral. On top of this, the spring at Harbaldown was the only one with a cave. It was a place where many pilgrims stopped and washed themselves before continuing their journey or pilgrimage on to Canterbury.

It had been a long day, and I needed to record the day's findings.

It was only after researching the history of the spring, that we realised the fresh spring water had served a hospital for lepers back in the Saxon times and had continued to do so through those later days of the Norman invasion on and beyond the days of the Black Prince.

The Ascent of Doubt

There was a problem, however. A friend who is a researcher of ancient roads and byways, and who is an expert in pilgrims' routes, pointed out to us that the ancient pilgrim's road was the main road from London to Canterbury, but it became very popular after the murder of Thomas à Becket. It was the death of the archbishop that popularised the route.

Our research took us back to the well and the time of the great resurgence of faith and contrition, when King Henry II made that famous 'crawl of a penitent' from the spring at Harbledown to the steps of Canterbury cathedral, after the death of Thomas à Becket.

It was said that a buckle from the shoe of Thomas à Becket was kept by the brothers of a holy place, a hospital built with money supplied by the archbishop Lanfranc in 1084, St Nicholas. It was here that this much-revered relic was kept, for the purpose of showing to travellers and pilgrims, and for them to admire and exchange the blessings they received from kissing the buckle in return for money, in the form of donations to the hospital.

We went back to our research and looked again at the original document from the 1390s. The reference to purifactory sacrifices Gurth spoke of was referring to events a hundred years before those days of Henry II. Harold would have been there long before the place became popular. We gave this some thought.

We looked again at the history of the place and found something surprising. Prior to the stone-built hospital funded by the archbishop Lanfranc, it was a wooden structure but was still a place where lepers were treated.

Rather than dampen our spirits, it made more sense of the old document. If the old road past the hospital had not been so popular in those days when Harold was there, which was, according to our calculation, around 1078–1085, would he not have been 'carrying out sacrifices of cleansing' for the benefit of the lepers rather than random pilgrims? Cleansing the feet of pilgrims would have been seen as 'ministering to', not 'cleansing'. The risk to health, washing, and cleansing the bodies of lepers could be seen as a sacrifice. This fresh look was important for us, because we were only too aware that it was possible to be lifted up with enthusiasm to the detriment of accurate research by moulding results from presumptions to suit our argument.

After going back to the research, we needed to ask a question. Were we in the right place? Was this the place Gurth mentioned while in conversation with Henry I?

Frances and I retreated into our studies to research.

St Nicholas Lepers Hospital

It became clear that this location was used as a place of both cleansing and healing. What of the reference Gurth made to the 'Rock'? Further research uncovered more. The name of this small town had, over the years, been spelt differently, including Harbaltown and Harbaldoun. Harbaldoun is a derivative of a medieval name taken from the growing of herbs there. Its former name in medieval times was Herbaltown. It was where herbs were grown for healing—so many varieties of herbs, in fact, that other herbalist came from all over the country to purchase the healing mixtures and balms.

The *Monthly Review*'s 1786 comments said,

> Herbaltown. It is a Town of the forest of Blean where Herbs of many varieties, some only found at Herbaltown, were sought by Herbals from every part of the country.

We knew we had to return, which we did the following week. The weather was inclement, and we found the old hospital closed. As we sat waiting for the curator to return, we talked about Harold and why he would have stopped at this location. Was there a particular reason why Harold would choose this place? We talked about the relationship he had with Edith the Fair. History tells us that after the battle, information about her whereabouts tended to be a little sketchy—in fact, nonexistent. We believed too that it would be pretty unlikely that we would discover any new evidence that could further our knowledge of her whereabouts after the conquest, because various historians who had searched for evidence, and the 'general consensus of opinion' was that she simply faded into obscurity.

There that phrase was again—'general consensus of opinion'. We decided we should look a little harder. We began to sift again through our research and eventually came upon searches we carried out in the area of the Marches, on the Welsh borders.

During our time in Shropshire, we had spoken to a local woman from Oswestry to uncover local tales about Harold. She told us that many times, her great grandmother had told her that their family were descendants of Harold. The family name was Northwood. The young woman had no idea whether or not this was true; she knew only that it was one of those things she remembered about her grandmother from when she was little. Her grandmother had always said that the family were descendants of Harold Godwin, 'the king'.

I asked Frances if she had checked this line of research, but she hadn't; it was pending further research. We dug out our reference works. It was a name and a lead, even though it seemed to be unlikely that this was anything more than a fancy, yet we had chased down fancies before. We take any claim seriously, and I know it's time-consuming, but it's how we get results. We began digging.

She had mentioned Kent. After many hours searching ancestry and family sites, we eventually came upon a family from Massachusetts. The researcher, a modern-day family member, had an extensive list from years of tracing family members, right back to an Alnod Cilt.

We had come across Cilt before. Following up on this lead, we discovered the family Norwood-Northwood, originally Norwode, was a name adopted by someone who purported to be the grandson of Harold. The name Norwode was taken from the name of the wood, North Wood.

This wood was behind an old manor close to the parish of Minster on the Isle of Sheppy, Kent. It was relevant, we believed, to establish any and all possible links to Harold because Gurth had made a reference to the family in one of the translations of the Latin text.

We discovered the Isle of Sheppy, and in particular Minster, was where Edith the Fair joined the nunnery after the battle. She had settled there and eventually died there. This could be important information because it was yet another piece of the puzzle, and it fitted with the testimony of Gurth, who was asked by Henry I what had happened to his brother, Harold.

Gurth referred to 'us' as in 'take the memory of him from us'. This could be a reference to us as being family. It could also mean that at some time through those years, Gurth was with the family at Sheppy too, and that Gurth and Edith knew that Harold was in Herbaltown, and that he then left there. Gurth explained that the family had heard no more until they heard he had spent time at a place near Chester and then sometime after had died in Chester. The parish of Minster, on the Isle of Sheppy, was but a day's journey to Herbaltown, so for a long period

Harold could have been staying just down the road from Gurth, his younger brother, and Edith, his handfasted wife.

With the evidence building, I feel tempted to drop the possibles, and maybes, for we were building a mighty case for the alternative story of Harold, the story according to the Englishmen.

Well of the Black Prince

The Limestone
Cave Herbaldown
circa 1086 AD

CHAPTER 10

There is a sketch of what the cave at Herbaltown would have looked like before it was walled up during the time of Edward III. It seems reasonable to assume that if many were getting to hear of Harold living as a hermit, news would get back to his family on Sheppy. We have Edith the Fair, who had moved away from Waltham to live as a nun at Minster on the isle of Sheppy, and she was finally buried in the old Minster, near her family manor.

Once we realised this, we felt it would be quite logical to assume Harold would have seen something of his family, even though this may have been carefully done. After all, as has been said, Sheppy was little more than a day's journey from Herbaltown. It seemed reasonable to assume so because of the way Gurth had chosen his words during his meeting with Henry I. He spoke of the family, or 'us', having knowledge of his 'appearing ... firstly in Canterbury'.

But before we move on, let's look at the wording of the Latin text. Gurth said, 'Changing his royal insignia for a dark grey garment.' How would Gurth have known this detail if he hadn't seen him? Why did he say in the original version, 'He [Harold] tried to take the memory of him from us'? Was this meant to include those lepers and nurses of Herbaltown, or did this also include his family? It seems likely to be so.

It was while we were in conversation about this family link and the possibility that Harold actually chose this place that we asked the question: Why choose this place, Herbaltown?

With the close proximity to his family in Sheppy and the wording Gurth used, it could mean that Harold had some contact with his family, with the distance to travel between the two places just a day's travelling. So why not stay on Sheppy, with his family?

It was while we were sitting in our car waiting for the rain to ease, parked outside the little church of St Nicholas in Herbaltown, that something occurred to us. Our conversation had just turned to the herb gardens that Herbaltown was famous for in Saxon times, and it was the ideal place for helping the sick. We chatted about the possible herbalist who ran the place. Who would have had such a diverse knowledge of exotic herbs? We both turned to each other.

The Saracen Nurse

'What if the herbalist is the Saracen nurse?' This simultaneous thought was born of pure optimism, and we immediately dismissed the preposterous suggestion, laughing. It was a crazy notion, but after all the many hours we had spent looking through so many manuscripts and documents, to glean just the smallest of snippets of information relative to the search that would move our investigation forward was not easy.

But then, to find any information on this mysterious nurse would be like finding ourselves falling into a virtual cave of gold and discovering the holy grail itself. It was simply not going to happen. Maybe in a Steven Spielberg film, but this was real life, so no! The idea was preposterous, but it gave us some amusement.

I smiled and shrugged, amused yet resigned as I reminded Frances of the comment from the translator of the Vita Haroldi, Walter De Grey Birch. 'Whether true or legendary, we may never know.' It was genuinely how we thought, and we had a realistic view of our prospects.

Researching events from so long ago could at times be very rewarding, but mostly it was a real grind, damned hard work to find any scraps, and with us looking back so far into Saxon times, if we did find some artefact that was significant, then we were lucky.

When the church curator eventually turned up, we borrowed the keys. The former hospital, now known as the Church of St Nicholas, is kept more as a museum these days. We entered the church. There are times during our research when we'd stumble into a moment, much like when a shambolic and indefinable shape you have wrestled with for so long, trying to understand, suddenly sheds that sloppy air and stands boldly before you. This day at Herbaltown was one such day.

Before I go any further, I need to explain why the subject of this mysterious Saracen nurse came to mind.

The Vita Haroldi

The Vita Haroldi speaks of a Saracen nurse, one skilled in the art of medicine, who found Harold and took him to Winchester, where she spent two years healing him of his wounds. These events were said to have taken place in a small cell beneath the church of Alfred. These events would not have taken place had Harold died on the field of battle, and this Saracen nurse would not have existed but in the mind of the writer who had contrived to invent these events.

If, however, these events actually took place, then our finding this nurse—but even more than finding her, discovering that there was such a person who was exactly as described in the Vita Haroldi, 'A Saracen nurse, skilled in the practice of medicine, and in the use of herbs'—would be the smoking gun that would begin to validate the contents of this forgotten myth and raise it up instead to being a plausible document that contains much more than hint of truthfulness within its pages.

It was as we wandered around the ancient hospital that we were taken by its atmosphere: dark, damp, yet still. Its history was of sickness and death, we could sense an almost palpable feeling of pain, and it was quite real. It was as if we were a part of some greater plan, and our purpose was one of apologists for a forgotten cause. We were searching almost without hope for some mark, some seemingly insignificant symbol, written centuries before by some unnamed, poor, condemned leprous soul who had been attended to by a former king.

We were drawn to an ancient, faded mural. It had been uncovered after years of being boarded over and protected. The window had been sealed for many years with boarding to protect the precious stained glass.

The church had a description for the murals, and the church called it 'The Annunciation'. IT featured Mary and the angel Gabriel.

I was puzzled. 'But the images are of two Black women!'

Frances agreed but, on reflection, reasoned, 'It's not unknown for artists in the past to use Black women as depicting Mary. But this is Canterbury.' Frances examined the women more closely and added, 'And not just that—look! The young one is holding an African feather fan!'

I looked closely, and it was true.

'When did you see a depiction of the angel Gabriel waving an African fan?' she asked.

It was difficult to make out much of the detail because the paintings, being so old, had flaked quite badly.

Herbaltown: Church of St Nicholas

We began trawling through the histories of the hospital and, after some research, found a description of the black lady as observed in 1758 by the reverend Bryan Faussett. We are truly grateful to him, for it describes the saintly lady in more detail through his eyes and description at a much earlier time, when the details in the paintings were much clearer.

> In the same Window is, also, the Figure of a Bishop (I suppose LANFRANC ye Founder) in a praying Posture. Also, the Figure of The Blessed Virgin, or some Female Saint, with a white Dragon at her Feet, a long Crosslet in her Left Hand, and something, like a Book, in her Right; and, underneath, this Fragment of an Inscription '… ella Capellan'.

This description did not include the young Black girl on the opposite reveal. Also, he acknowledged that the true identity of the woman was not known. He had called her the Virgin Mary or some saintly woman!

In the years that followed this description given by Reverend Faussett, some of the detail was lost, and, as the paint peeled and the colours faded, it would appear the two forgotten ladies were posthumously awarded the title 'Mary and Gabriel:. The Annunciation'.

I disagree with the description, but only because it seems to me that if in 1758, the historian Reverend Faussett was not sure, then for the hospital to call them the Virgin Mary and the angel Gabriel, it's clear that the identity of these two ladies is still unknown.

I would offer another identity for the two. There are clues in the paintings—necessary clues for us today because by the time Reverend Faussett recorded his description, the memory of them had been forgotten. The older of the two women is carrying a small book; by her feet is a white dragon, or wyvern, and her title is Elle Capellan. The younger woman on the opposite reveal has red hair and is dressed as a Moorish woman of the twelfth century, as is the older woman.

Had these images been of Moorish or Saracen doctors, and men, who were well-known in the Middle Ages to be especially skilled in surgical and healing techniques, I doubt even then that these would be named and remembered.

England was entering a time of fear, of piety, and of church-run hospitals. The Normans had arrived. The methods these skilled foreigners used appeared to the common people to be in many ways miraculous. The church and those who ran those very Christian establishments back then were suspicious of any healers who did not adhere to those accepted methods adopted by the fathers, and when prayers and contrition were not used as an important part of the process of healing, then some began to blame 'other darker forces' as to why healing was taking place, because it was believed there could be no successful healing unless prayers and contrition were included in the care of the sick.

The success of herbalists and healers was viewed by some as bordering on witchcraft and messing with the black arts. There were stories that came back from the Crusades, not long after these times where healers, skilled Arab and Moorish surgeons and 'potion makers', were accused by Christian monks of doing the devil's work. These monks, because they had no skills medically, and who were amputating limbs because of infection, called these doctors wicked and engaged in the devil's work, because their potions 'magically' stopped infection, saved limbs, and cured the sick. Even today there are still some who question the benefits of herbal medicine.

On the following page, if you look closely, the book she is holding has a symbol in the centre similar to an ornate M. The book widely accepted by Arabic, Jewish, and Moorish doctors in the eleventh and twelfth centuries as the handbook for the healer and surgeon was titled *Medici* and written by a first-century doctor who wrote down his learnings anonymously. Another symbol used by the unknown painter is the use of the mandrake flower, another ancient symbol for healing.

We should examine also the white dragon at her feet. This we will look more closely at.

The young girl has red hair and a North African feather fan. There is clearly a difference in ages, and both women are facing each other, indicating that they were associated and that there was a personal connection of sorts.

The older woman holding the book has been given the title Elle Capellan, a title Moorish in origin, and the female equivalent to the English title chaplain. This at the time was unusual because the position of a chaplain was normally assigned to a man, although some duties could be carried out by women. However, this was a Saracen woman whose very appointment meant that she was well respected, and although the hospital was small, she had status.

We will look at and examine all these points and determine the place these women have in relation to the Vita Haroldi and our search.

CHAPTER 11

I know I've used the analogy of a Lancashire hotpot before, but for a Lancashire lass to create a Lancashire hotpot then, she would use all the ingredients needed, and when it is consumed, those eating it would identify it as a Lancashire hotpot. Let's see if all this new information makes sense in relation to the search for answers about Harold.

The original title of the woman is Elle Capellan, which is Spanish for The Chaplain (female). The woman and her younger companion were Spanish or, as those from this area in the eleventh century were known, Moors. The population of Spain at that time was a mixture of Arabic Muslim, Jewish, and Christian. This lady could have been Saracen or a Moor, a Christian or a Muslim. We have the best description through the eyes of the reverend who was looking at a much clearer image than we can today, so every piece of information is important.

The small book she is holding was not noted or recognised by Reverend Faussett as a Bible, and we accept that he clearly had a better look at the details than we can. Yet it was painted in as a symbol of some important reference or an indication of her work or skills. In view of the size and the plainness of the covering, it is unlikely to be a prayer book or a book of some religious significance. In view of the very nature of the good work carried out there and the fact that this place was known for its many varieties of healing plants and herbs then, it seems likely to be a book on herbal medicines and remedies.

The Vita Haroldi talks of a Saracen nurse skilled in the use of herbs, and this place, as it was known in those early days, was Herbaltown—the name of Harbaldown in the eleventh century. This was the very centre of medicine in Saxon times, where herbals (herbalists) would travel to from all over England to seek a wider variety of herbs, plants, and remedies not readily available in England yet needed for healing. Is it not logical to say that any of those loyal to Harold would have known exactly whom to call—someone who would have the skills needed to heal his wounds? Is it no different today to say if any of our royals fell seriously ill, then the right doctors with the best skills would be summoned?

St Nicholas, Herbaltown, was not a church but a hospital for the lepers. Lepers in those times were not cast out but helped, even by those who held high positions in society. This place was so well-known for its importance medically that Henry I donated land to help Lanfranc, the archbishop of Canterbury, pay for the building of the original stone-built hospital, and later Henry II paid towards its upkeep.

This St Nicholas Hospital was one of the first of the country's leper hospitals, and during this time, another was set up in the cells and small rooms under the Saxon Abbey at Winchester. A nurse familiar with leprosy and with the skills to treat it may have been a frequent traveller along the pilgrim road from Canterbury to Winchester, little more than a day's travelling in those times. What I find interesting is that in the Vita Haroldi, it mentions nothing of lepers being treated in the cells or dark, cell-like places under the old abbey where Harold was cured. It states only that when it was suggested to Harold he be moved to a better, more suitable place, he insisted he stay in those cells. We don't know whether this would have been where the treatment of those with leprosy would have been. It could have been later, because those infected returned from the Crusades in greater numbers, or because leprosy was known and being treated in England a long time before these days, the small cells below ground in these religious houses could have been where some were treated before better facilities were established through the church.

Now that we have a little more insight, this gives us a greater understanding of what was going on behind the scenes during these times. Some matters were not expanded on by the writer of the Vita Haroldi, maybe because he did not know! Whether the thoughts of Harold so early after his army's defeat was one of penitence or a seeking of the grace of God, or whether this a clever place for the defeated king to hide and be cured, is for speculation. We do know that later, it is said he was filled with remorse and lived out his life as a penitent.

The White Wyvern

Looking again at the images in St Nicholas Hospital, the white dragon said to be at her feet is interesting. If, as in ancient symbolism, the dragon is featured, it is not sat beside a holy personage, and it is under their feet to denote a dominance over evil. In this wall painting, the wyvern is sat beside her like a pet. Also, it is not normal to depict the dragon as white (the symbolic colour of purity) but red or brown.

The symbol on Harold's battle banner was a white or golden wyvern, or dragon. A white wyvern is also the symbol of the house of Wessex.

CHAPTER 12

Although this building is called St Nicholas, it is helpful to remember that its history is that of a hospital and not a church. I mention this because the wall paintings reflect some of the history of the building. If we examine some of the known characters, like Lanfranc, an image depicting Jesus, and there is the depiction of the last judgement—all images with a strong connection to the early history of the hospital—then it is no surprise that a capellan, or female chaplain, and her young assistant or daughter should be featured, and quite prominently.

The age of this wall is recorded as around 1190, the time of Henry II. The age of the paintings are said to be later by a hundred years or so, however I believe they date back further, to around the same period. One reason why they are likely earlier is because the memories of those women had been forgotten by the fourteenth century, because there are no records to confirm who they were. For them to have been so highly thought of so as to be immortalised, I believe these paintings would have had to have been completed not too long after their lives had ended.

The possible explanation as to why these images would have survived so well is because these have only recently been uncovered. For many years, the end wall has been covered to protect the stained-glass windows. The result of this has been of benefit to the paintings, which still show many features that would have been lost through ageing.

The dating of the paintings of this period can be cross-checked with similar paintings, but it is also important to understand that these wall paintings are of a time period. The subjects are by an unknown artist who completed these images during a set period of time.

We have an image of Lanfranc, who was in office as the archbishop of Canterbury, till 1089. It was he who donated to the building of this, the first of the stone-built hospitals for lepers. There are also depictions of the poor, tormented souls who suffered their diseases in this place, and with the absence of other notable contributors to this hospital who came along after the demise of Lanfranc, we could deduce that this homage in the form of wall art was primarily for those important people who helped to establish this institution back in the early twelfth century.

We know of Lanfranc and that he was late eleventh century, but then we have the two women! Presumably they are from the same period, into the twelfth century.

Let's look for a moment at the other painting, the young black girl with the cheeky smile and a large feather fan. She is depicted as a young girl with red hair and is dressed in style of clothing as the older woman, in the dress of a Saracen or Moor. The angel Gabriel? No, I don't think so.

Unless, that is, the angel Gabriel is occasionally depicted as a young black girl with a large feather fan and a cheeky smile!

A Look at the Timeless Bond Formed
between a Patient and His Nurse

We don't have to venture back into history to find this. Sometimes and inevitable bond forms between nurse and patient. There are many examples of a strong bond forming in such circumstances. According to the Vita Haroldi, Harold was with this Saracen nurse for two years. He had serious battle damage and a need for infection control, surgery, blood-loss treatment, and likely bone-setting skills. He was thought to have been born between 1022 and 1026, so in he was his early to mid-forties, and he no doubt had her complete trust, and she his. In those two years, they would have undoubtedly become close.

Could this young girl, who was honoured by being pictured opposite the older woman, and who clearly seems to be unskilled, in fact be her daughter? Red hair? Age around fifteen? I believe this young lady, from her appearance and taking into consideration that there are no titles attributed to her actual image, is Harold's daughter.

Of course it's conjecture on my part, and I could be misreading the symbolisms within the paintings. These images of our two ladies reveal a lot, as we have seen. It's important to remember that during this period of our history, there are no references to skilled female doctors, and unless you were a woman of royal decent or a high-born, you would not be recognised, especially, if you were a Moor or a Saracen woman. Therefore for these women to be so honoured by being included in a selection of wall paintings alongside the likes of Lanfranc, these women were very special.

In the eleventh century, the most skilled people practising medicine were the surgeons from the Arab world, and although this was widely accepted as a man's work, women worked as surgeons and healers too. Often these women were more advanced and skilled than some of the men. I believe this woman is the herbalist who dispensed herbal remedies and medicine, and because of the way women were viewed at the time, we do not expect to find this healer in any writings of that age.

A Certain Rock

The reference to the meeting with Henry I as told to us by Gurth, Harold's younger brother, was that after the battle, Harold first appeared in Canterbury at some 'certain rock'. Further research uncovered some ancient references to this time: that because of its importance as a place of healing, and a place where lepers could go to be treated, it was ordered by Henry I that the hill upon which the hospital of St Nicholas stood should be stripped of all shrubs, bushes, and trees so that the limestone would be exposed. This was done, and during those times, according to ancient documents, the town stood out for miles around for all to see and was known locally as 'the rock'.

When Gurth was asked by Henry I about the validity of the story in reference to the escape of Harold, and Gurth spoke of this 'certain rock', he knew that Henry I knew this place for Henry I had donated a parcel of land to it and had prayed for the good health of his wife there.

In William Somner's *Antiquities of Canterbury*, it gives the agreement by Henry I to donate ten perches of land (165 feet) on every side of the hospital of St Nicholas, Herbaltown, 'for the saving of his and Maud's souls', to have the brothers of that hospital grub up and clear all around the hill that the hospital stood on, and to expose the whole hill for the purpose of showing to all this special place (vol. 1, p. 46).

It is interesting to note that Harbaldown is built on limestone, and from early images in seventeenth-century paintings of this place, it shows the white limestone, after six hundred years, still showing around the hospital. There is no doubt in my mind that when Gurth spoke of 'a certain rock near Canterbury', Henry I knew this place as the leper hospital known as St Nicholas in the forest of Bleane. For Gurth to mention this to Henry I, it may have been a declaration of his brother's obvious piety, and it added some value to his character in those days.

Harold's Fame

How long Harold stayed at this spring performing acts of cleansing, we do not know; the period of ten years was mentioned in the Vita Haroldi. We cannot be certain, but it was certainly long enough for news of his being there to spread so that many from near and far came to spend time with him.

Why did Harold stay so long in this place? A desire for absolution? An opportunity to display a penitent spirit? A desire to do good works because of the hardships his losing to William would have caused? These may have been part of it.

Also, this was close to where his brother Gurth and Edith, his handfasted wife, were, and of course his youngest son by Edith the Fair, just a day's journey from Herbaltown to Sheppy. It is also where the Saracen nurse was based, so he was with family, people for whom he had affection. Would his spending time with the nurse who healed him, and even helping her as she worked amongst the poor and destitute, have been a way in which he could pay her something back? I like to think so.

Review

The reference from the Latin document of the meeting between Gurth and Henry I says the following.

> He [Harold] first appeared openly, in the cave of a certain rock, near Canterbury, in which he lived as a hermit, performing several purificatory sacrifices. But,

since his fame was starting to spread, a considerable number of people, from both far, and near, began spending time with him, to such an extent, that he strove to take away any memory of himself among them/us.

Here's what we found at Herbaltown. We found a spring near Canterbury where there was, back in the eleventh century, a cave by the spring. We found that this place was used for sacrifices of cleansing, it was called locally 'the rock', it was a centre for herbs and medicines, and it was known as the place to buy herbal remedies by virtually all of England at the time. We know that the woman who is depicted holding a medicine book, or a book of herbal remedies, was honoured for her work as a healer. She was a Moor or a Saracen, and she had a daughter (we believe).

We know that St Nicholas Hospital was well-known, and possibly the first stone-built leper hospital to be purpose-built, and that soon after its construction, places for treating lepers sprung up in the North as well as in Winchester and London, spreading across the country. We know that in Saxon times, the pilgrims travelled to and from Canterbury to Winchester, and it was a little more than a day on the pilgrim road in the eleventh century.

This makes a case for the Vita Haroldi and the account that Harold was healed by a Saracen nurse after the battle. The fact that this black woman, known as Elle Chaplain, was loved enough to be honoured by having her image painted alongside the likes of Lanfranc, and the Virgin Mary, it's likely she was loved for her work with the sick and, after considering those symbols that seem to connect Harold to that place, for her healing Harold, their king.

Is it not reasonable to assume the Saracen nurse would have worked in both places, bearing in mind their close proximity? Or was the reference made by the sagas, that after the battle Harold was taken to Canterbury, true? This is not fully established.

I also think it worth asking the question, What possible reasons would the scribes who recorded these events back in the 1300s have to lie about the meeting and the matters discussed between Henry I and the younger brother of Harold? Was there monetary or political gain to be had? I would very much doubt that a story like this one, which would have to be so well researched so as to be able to irrefutably prove beyond doubt that each short reference written in a spurious statement, given by a supposed brother of the old king should be questioned amidst fear of it being disputed, would stand up as plausible. The notion is preposterous!

Also, this report that Harold survived the battle was repeated in separate documents at the time, one of which was entered into a manuscript that was hidden for four hundred years! Therefore we have, even today, the thoughts of eminent historians who repeat what the previous generation of historians say, and so on, that without evidence we must assume the story that Harold escaped the battle in 1066 is a myth, and those reports from eyewitnesses must be discounted because so many more chroniclers have said Harold and his brother Gurth died.

CHAPTER 13

Next, this may seem trivial in light of the evidence already gathered, but I think I should make some comment on the seemingly extraordinary longevity of Harold and Gurth. Both references to the end of Gurth's and Harold's lives came in or around their ninetieth year. At the time of Gurth meeting Henry I at Woodstock, it was twelve years after Harold's death in Chester.

It's worth noting that, in the 'histories of Harbaldown and St Nicholas,' you can read of the life spans of the early brothers who were buried there. The ages of the majority were said to be well beyond the four score years, making them on average well over eighty years of age. This is testament to the treatment and diet those humble souls received there.

This is important information, because many people in our times have a misconception that in the Middle Ages, people's life expectancy was no more than forty. Although this was true in many places where famine and pestilence were rife, in establishments where one received treatments from the church, as a pilgrim or a hermit, or in the care of the chaplains, one lasted much longer.

These places where pilgrims and hermits spent time had their own orchards and vegetable gardens, with chicken houses and pigs. Many had ovens for baking fresh bread and pies, and there was cheese, milk, and butter. They were separate from the villages, although the fathers would take some of their produce to assist the elderly or infirm in the local area. These establishments were well stocked and were healthy places to stay.

Gurth was himself approaching the end of his life when he met Henry I at Woodstock, being around ninety years of age—a great age, as was Harold—and like his brother before him, he dressed as a hermit yet was still a 'tall man of elegant stature'. There is an occasion mentioned in a certain document about the supposed brother of Harold meeting Henry II. This obviously could not have happened because Henry II did not appear until much later.

I say again that I find it difficult to believe Gurth would feel the need to lie to the king, and on such an important point. Why would he? He would be his own man who would have no need of agendas. He was a holy man who must have carried a fair amount of remorse and regret around and who hopefully found peace at the end of a long life. Why would he lie?

It appears from the translation we examined that Gurth had argued with his brother, King Harold, and had tried to persuade him to wait, to withdraw from the battlefield before the battle had commenced. We also have the testimony from Master Wace, and it seems to me that Gurth had tried to reach his brother's side when Harold was beaten to the ground. It tells us that Gurth was himself beaten down and did not rise again.

It was assumed by the chroniclers that they both died together, yet we have this testimony from Gurth, as an old man and hermit, in conversation with Henry I in 1124! So he obviously survived too. There have been no documents referencing Gurth from 1066 onward, just the meeting in Woodstock, Oxfordshire, and the meeting at Waltham Abbey around the same time.

I can only surmise that rather than die alongside Leofric, his brother, that day as history would have us believe, he made his escape to lead a solitary life, and in the end, he finished his days as a hermit like his brother Harold. This little snapshot of Harold and Gurth is unique, piecing together an event on which secular history has no information.

I believe that in view of the close proximity of where the two brothers fell together, and discerning that, Gurth as an older man at Woodstock, was seemingly sound in body and health, that he was able to recover from the blows that rendered him unconscious on the battlefield, like his brother Harold. Possibly he was amongst those of Harold's people who helped get Harold to Winchester.

In retrospect, Gurth was right. His advice to withdraw was a sound tactic, knowing the strength of William's army and knowing how tired

Harold and his men were. They had only to hold and wait two days, and then the fleet already on its way and heading into the channel and reinforcements would have joined them. Yet it did not hold Gurth back from loyally following his brothers into battle.

We are examining the life of Harold after the battle in this book, and how the destruction of his kingdom pained him. But I must make mention of Gurth, who had fought bravely alongside his brother at Stamford Bridge and at Senlac Hill. He did not join other surviving members of his family in battling on against the Norman invasion; like Harold, he seemed to accept the loss as God's will.

The fact that at the age he was, in 1124 AD, around 90, to still be wearing the Lorica, (Chain mail) as was the same with Harold, this may well have been an act of penitence, a sign of contrition.

The search continues with Harold in Herbaltown. Due to the growing number of people from near and far away coming to where he was performing these 'cleansing sacrifices', he moved away to avoid the attention. Before examining the next phase of his journey, I would like to mention a method used by the authorities when dealing with escapees—people who have, for one reason or another, gone into hiding.

My wife, who worked inside the military, wanted us to employ a modern tactic used to good effect by the professionals. It's quite often the case that when fugitives go to ground, they will find places they are familiar with—old haunts, girlfriends, family, and areas they know. We looked at this when looking at the travels of Harold, and there is a similar pattern. Although it is true that I believe Harold did not consider himself a fugitive, he could well have had places he would visit that he was familiar with, or where folks whom he knew lived.

CHAPTER 14

Shropshire

I accepted quite early on in this search that very little physical evidence would come to light, and it was well-known that in Saxon times. very little documentation existed. The Saxons were not note takers. It has taken many months of sifting through ancient documents to make the progress we have made because apart from *The Anglo-Saxon chronicles*, very little was written about the events of the time that were not part of the mainstream recorded histories. Those ordinary folks who witnessed their old king in either Canterbury or Cheswardine would have been illiterate or loyal to Harold, and the chances of finding written accounts of Harold being seen are few. The fact that we have found documents where these extraordinary events occurred is testament to our thorough research. After having made some progress, I believe this is an indication that there must be other evidence we have not yet come across, and maybe never will.

When I found the references to Harold's life after the battle, I wanted to test the authenticity of the documents when it came to the details, even when looking at the seemingly insignificant details like the geographical locations. Were they in harmony with Harold's history? Were there connections not mentioned in the documents?

As the writer of the Vita Haroldi who was being told of this journey through the notes of the old servant of Harold, Sebricht, I would assume Sebricht would not have given explanations as to why Harold went on the journey he did. If he had done, then this would have ended up in the script of the Vita Haroldi, because the document indeed, carries a narrative beyond the succinct. It seems he simply related what had happened on that journey.

We looked at the places Harold travelled to from the military perspective of someone going to ground, as has been suggested by Frances, my wife. Let's test the authenticity of this tale with this in mind.

Let's Go on a Manhunt!

Were there connections to Harold in any of these places? Was it reasonable to accept the possibility that an ex king of the Saxons would feel drawn, for whatever reasons, to these locations? I spent some considerable time in the Marches of Shropshire, and it occurred to me that a way to describe my findings was with the same analogy I used earlier: the old hotpot.

If stew is served you with all the ingredients of a Lancashire hotpot, then the likelihood is it's a Lancashire hotpot.

I mention this analogy again because when I retraced the journey of Harold, taken from the document, I found a number of connections to Harold. The Vita Haroldi did not elaborate as to why it mentioned these locations. Maybe it was because, as I've already said, the writer was told only where these locations were and not why Harold travelled there.

I'd like to make an observation at this point in reference to the Vita Haroldi. It is quite wordy, and the writer spoke of times and events he was made aware of, but Harold spent very little of this period in Cheswardine.

I believe the writer was told of these locations but had no more information as to why Harold spent time there, and because he did not know, I reiterate it only because I feel this is key to testing whether the Vita Haroldi is lying. If this was an attempt by some dishonest troublemaker from the twelfth century to write a fancy or a fairy tale, then in mentioning Cheswardine, he would surely have then gone on to explain whom Harold knew from these parts or why Harold travelled here. He didn't.

However, I came to realise after much research that it would have been quite logical that Harold would have made his way here. Why? Because he was familiar with these places.

Cheswardine was as a location Harold knew well. Where is Cheswardine? Cheswardine is an ancient town in north-east Shropshire. If we examine the connection this town has with Harold, it may help us to understand that this was not a random choice for Harold; it was not simply somewhere to escape to after being recognised in Herbaltown.

This was an area he knew well, so we can confidently conclude it is an area where he spent time both during and after the conflicts of 1063 when, as Edward's earl and head of the English army, he assaulted the Welsh, quashing their rebellions.

There was a distinguished family who had owned Cheswardine and the surrounding manors: Leofric, Earl of Mercia. This was the husband of Godgifu (Godiva), who famously pleaded with her husband to lower the crippling taxes on the people of Coventry and who was challenged by her husband to ride naked through the streets of Coventry to test the depth of her compassion for the people. This she did, but before she undertook this task, she implored the people to close their shutters and clear the streets in order to spare her shame.

It was her granddaughter, the former queen of the Welsh king Gruffydd ap Llywelyn, whom Harold married after the Welsh king's death.

The Grandsons of Godgifu, Earls Morcar and Edwin, were the first to confront Tostig, the brother of Harold, and Haraald the Viking in the north, just prior to the Battle at Stamford Bridge. Earlier, in the days when Harold was earl to King Edward, there was animosity between Leofric and the Godwins, but by the time Harold became king, things had changed. The two grandsons of Leofric were loyal to Harold. It is true, that by the time Harold had made this journey to Cheswardine, Edwin had been killed, and there is a possibility that Morcar was still in prison in Winchester. Even so, this was an area with which Harold was familiar.

There are no records we could find to say that his wife, Edith the Black, was in the vicinity at the time. We have only the request from her brother, after the battle in 1066, that for her safety and that of her and Harold's child, she should move north to live near Chester, which is a day's travel from Cheswardine. It is recorded that she died around 1086 and was buried in Coventry. This is, from our calculations, around the same time Harold journeyed to Cheswardine.

There is also the son of Harold by Edith the Black, also called Harold. What happened to him? We know from history that young Harold had travelled to Norway and had been welcomed by the king, who then praised his father, Harold II, because Harold had shown honour to their family by sparing his life as the son of Harald Hardrada. He was just sixteen at the time. Harold had allowed him to return with what was left of his father's army.

When Harold's son, also named Harold, travelled on this journey, he was no more than eighteen at the time, which would mean that the year would have been 1084. He joined with Magnus King of Norway and fought with him against established Viking strongholds in the Orkneys, the Isle of Mann, Anglesey, and Ireland.

It's interesting that around the time Harold was in Cheswardine, this was around the time no more was heard from his son on the world scene. For that matter, neither was anything heard from Edith, Harold's second wife. Personally, I like to think that Harold, in true fugitive style, had gone to ground with Edith and his son, if only briefly. Even if this was not so, Harold would know places where a simple pilgrim named Christian and his young companion, Moses, could find shelter, and where there would still be a loyal Saxon or two. He would likely have moved around because at the time, there were still Saxons living in those parts.

His former estates at Weston were not a half day's walk from Cheswardine. This whole area would have been familiar to him. If he had need of a place to stay, he would have known the hermit's place at Hadnal, opposite the church his father had built. He would have known of the ancient Saxon well with healing waters just across from what is now Haughmond Abbey. But there was a problem!

Others would know Harold: the families of the Welsh who had suffered from the results of Harold's war against the Welsh.

This was the Marches. The Welsh also lived close to here, and he was not totally unrecognisable, as was borne out from his experiences while living in Herbaltown. Cloth mask or no, it would be only a matter of time before a Welsh local with a grudge would remember him, and so it transpired to be. After a number of beatings and occasions when he was robbed of some articles of clothing, Harold moved on, this time on to Chester.

Before we are accused of cherry-picking the information we use, I'd like to comment on the hard work of some of our early historians. While Darwin, the English naturalist, was commenting on his own work and findings, he made the point that 'should more understanding, and light be shed on nature's genetics, in the future, then I would expect that my theory of natural selection would likely collapse'. He was right to accept the fact that theories that worked in those times don't fare so well in our scientific world.

Like the historians I have referred to as being mistaken regarding their prognosis in certain areas, we still need their eyes because they write down their findings, whether or not they believe the information. It is important, researched information, and historians and archaeologists today, with the benefit of more advanced technology, can reopen their research and examine it more closely.

Here are areas around Cheswardine with which Harold would have been familiar.

- The Saxon well at Haughmond Hill was said to have healing powers. The stone housing was built later but stands over the original spring.
- The church at Hadnal, built by his father, Earl Godwineson, and the hermitage opposite.
- The small Manor of Western, given him by Edwin, Earl of Mercia. After the battle in 1066, this manor came to be inhabited by a largely Welsh contingent. This may explain the harassment Harold was said to have endured at the hands of the Welsh, as recorded in the Vita Haroldi.

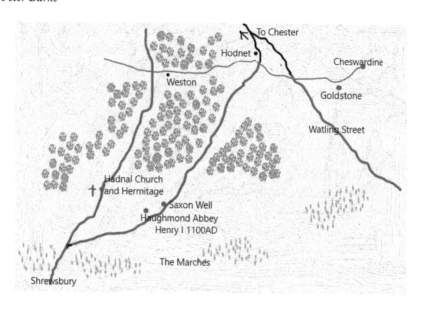

The Saxon Well

The Saxon Well

PTBURKE 18

CHAPTER 15

Chester

I make reference to Reverend Daniel and Samuel Lysons. Although this father and son team were inclined towards the generally accepted opinion that Harold died in 1066, they travelled to Chester in the early 1800s to gather information from the people of Chester as to the story of the Chester Hermit. Locals told them it was common knowledge in Chester that while Henry I was travelling back from Wales, he was told of the hermit of St James, and of the people's suspicions as to the hermit's identity. The father and son team were told by the locals that Henry I visited Harold in his cell at St James, and a secret but protracted conversation took place.

Could this have been true? More interesting, though, could this have been the motive behind Henry I asking Harold's brother in 1124, 'Were the rumours true? Did your brother survive the slaughter?'

Let's briefly go over the series of events. Dates are from 1068 to 1069.

After two years being healed by the Saracen nurse, Harold travelled abroad in an attempt to raise support from the dukes of Saxony and Germany. Having failed to secure support, he travelled, possibly on a pilgrimage to the holy land. Sometime during this absence from England, he stopped trying to gather support in raising an army and began to feel remorse. He began calling himself Christian and travelled in the guise of a pilgrim. Somewhere during this time, he found a companion called Moses. Was this person Christian, Jewish, or Muslim? The Vita Haroldi does not say. It was some years later when he appeared near Canterbury, and from there he travelled on to the Marches of Shropshire, and later on to other places.

What would life on the road have been like for Harold and his companion in those days? Based on the politics of this time period, around 1080–1090, William I would have still been alive for the first part of this decade, and he had been in France contesting with his son Robert for the power to rule. William also had rebellion in the north of England to deal with.

William I returned to England for two years while his eldest son, Robert Cuthrose, during an uneasy peace with his father, was sent to Scotland to repel Malcolm, the king of Scotland. As a pilgrim with a companion, Harold would have been travelling from parish to parish and been cared for, as was customarily the case for a Christian pilgrim. He would have been fed and given a place to sleep by the church. He covered his face with a cloth when he met company on the road.

I can't help but feel that in terms of quality of life, Harold had become a free man in so many ways. While William, his former adversary, was committed to building his own empire and was under constant threat and stress, here we have the former king, Harold, living a far holier and calmer life.

It is worth mentioning at this juncture that there was a great deal of importance given at the time to the consideration of one's need of godly acts of penitence due to humans' natural sinful tendencies. This pairs with the superstitions that still affected most all Normans and Saxons alike, who still felt tied to some of the pagan gods of the past.

Throughout the Christian calendar, there were strong connections to their old pagan ways; actually, these still exist today. Christmas was also Yule, the celebrations of the newborn sun, when Odin would ride across the skies and visit Saxons and Vikings in their homes. Odin the wise, all-knowing, fatherly man had an eight-legged horse, Sleipner, and brought good cheer to all in their homes on one special night. Sound familiar?

Eostre was the goddess of fertility, eggs, bunnies, and the like; in the Christian world, this time was Easter. Lammas was the loaf mass, the feast of the first fruits. For Christians, this was the harvest festival.

It is understandable that some events that befell those Saxons back then would be seen as signs, omens, and portents, because they had merely crossed over the road in terms of styles of worship, and most had followed the same traditions of their forefathers in pagan worship.

The appearance of the comet we today know as Halley's comet, which appeared in 1066, would have been seen by many as an omen. William's barbarism that saw the massacre of so many innocent people, and the harrowing of the North, Harold could have seen as a fulfilment of the prophecy told him by Edward the king before he died. It could be that by the time Harold had left Herbaltown in Kent, William had died, and his second son, William Rufus, was on the throne. This would have been around 1088. As discussed earlier, before the Norman invasion, Harold owned the manor of Western, near Cheswardine; his new brothers-in-law, Earls Morcar and Edwin, were from there; his second wife, Edith the Black, was from there; and maybe at the time of his return, possibly his son, Harold, the son he had never met, could have returned from his travels by then.

It is common knowledge that Harold was superstitious; for example, he believed after praying to the holy cross that he had been healed by its magical powers. When travelling down from defeating Harald Hardrada and the Vikings at Stamford Bridge, he stopped and prayed at the holy cross before continuing on to Sanlac Hill to face William.

In Shropshire, not five miles south of the place in which the Vita Haroldi manuscript says Harold stayed as a hermit, there is an ancient well with healing properties, said to have been used in Saxon times. It is next to what is now known as Haughmond Abbey.

When we asked locals if they had any stories about those ancient times, one story came up a couple of times. It has been told that 'the king', near death from an arrow wound, was cured using honey. Another, out of Oswestry, said that they had been told he was brought to the Marches by his friends but died there. These stories were not borne of the same night in a local pub, in conversation with a group of locals. They were from unconnected sources.

Let's take the first: that he was cured with honey. We know today of the effectiveness of honey as an antiseptic and a healer. This method as treatment would have been effective back then.

The next story was that his friends brought him up after the battle, but he died here. This belief came from a local source, but let's look at events from a local perspective. If this story has been passed down from old tales from who knows where, can we make a connection between local Shropshire tales and the events of that time according to the Vita Haroldi?

The Vita Haroldi states, 'Harold, being continually assaulted by the Welsh, who recognised him from the wars he waged against the Welsh, under King Edward, left that place, and after being given a sign, made his way to Chester.' If we had lived in the Marches in those times, and we knew or had heard the gossip that the old king was there and was being assaulted by the Welsh, but then we heard later that he had disappeared, what would most people conclude? We may conclude that he had survived the battle somehow, a friend had brought him up to the Marches, but then he had died of his injuries.

We have a period of time he was said to have been in the area, but another question arises. Why travel so close to a place known to you as being heavily populated with Welsh, a place where you and your brother Tostig brutally massacred Welsh rebels by the hundreds, maybe thousands, during the Welsh border wars in 1062-1063? This is something more to do with balancing the books, I would guess. Of course, we cannot overplay conjecture, but as a way of tying up this section in a neat bow and moving on, let's look at some later examples.

Royalty's Attitudes towards Penitence

Let's discuss Henry II and Thomas à Becket. Henry's need for penitence is clearly seen in the concessions he made to the church after the murder of Thomas, as well as his flagellations in public while crawling from Herbaltown to Canterbury. We also have the actions of Queen Matilda, who kissed the feet of the lepers in penitence so as to assure her place in heaven.

We may struggle to understand the mindset of the people of those times, but clearly they strongly felt a need for forgiveness and earning God's grace.

Another possibility is his estate at Weston, according to local church records, was well populated by the Welsh. It is possible that Harold travelled through his old manor to look over it and was recognised.

It is a problem as a modern writer, having read through the Vita

Haroldi and trying to understand the mood of the period, to explain the feelings of Harold and the regret he must have felt not just at the loss of his kingdom but also of the trouble and persecution it had brought to the Saxon people. Could he have thought that his being scourged during those times may have been a form of just punishment, accepted as part of his penitence? We don't know.

CHAPTER 16

The search took me finally to Chester, or Cestrae. There is more historically here than simply reading from the Vita Haroldi. I see the history from this place as separate from the history contained in the Vita Haroldi. Chester has its own stories about Harold the hermit.

There is an old story around the church of St John and the cemetery of St James next door. The old Anchorite cell, said to be where Harold's hermit cell was, was carved out of the sandstone rock. There is said to be a ghost who walks the city walls and around the old church of St John in the early hours. It is an apparition who is said to be heard mumbling in a strange language; some believe it is Saxon. It is a tall figure in a grey cloak. Some say it's the old hermit, Harold, the last Saxon king.

The tutor of young Richard I and King John, Gerald of Wales, a half Norman and half Welshman, was of good character and well respected. He relates in his histories that he was informed about the hermit of St James and that Harold had escaped the battle badly injured and sought refuge in St James, Chester. Other references speak of Harold's body being buried behind the altar of St Nicholas at St John's Church, Chester.

Brompton, and Knighton

Various sources make mention of Harold after the battle. One such was from inside the court of Malcolm, king of Scotland. Aelred of Rievaulx's comment is worth pondering: 'Whether Harold died a wretched death, or lived out his days as a penitent as some say …' It is clear that Aelred was familiar with the account of Harold as a penitent. Aelred was well travelled, and in his later life, he was not too far from Chester; this was some twenty-five years after the said death of Harold in 1112.

'As some say.' Aelred had also heard the stories of Harold. It always gives me cause to pause, as they say, when a recorder of history sees worth it to mention as part of his records a 'possibility'.

Aelred of Rievaulx

As a young man, Aelred had lived in the court of the king of Scotland. Is it reasonable to assume this doubt he had about Harold came from hearing rumours inside the court, possibly an accounting of the testimony of Gurth at Woodstock, bearing in mind that Henry I's wife, Matilda, who was of Saxon nobility, was from the same castle? News of that meeting—that Harold lived on after the battle as a penitent and later died living as a hermit—would have reached the castle.

It is worth repeating that the writer of the Vita Haroldi gained most of his information from the former companion of Harold, Sebricht. The canon or monk from Harold's abbey at Waltham, who wrote of these events at the time, spoke of the godly stature of Sebricht and his being loyal to Harold and honest in all his ways. The Vita Haroldi was kept safe and hidden at Waltham Abbey for four hundred years, its existence known only by those faithful monks. Yet this story of Harold's survival, and these self-same details of his movements during those years after the battle, are the same. Interesting too that these stories, even from the Norse sagas, where tales from history are sometimes embellished, speak of the Harold of those times as a penitent and holy man, contrite and humble—not heroic, as in leading bands of rebels slaughtering the evil murderous Normans.

It is known and accepted by historians that although the oral tales of the Norwegians and Scandinavians were not copied down in written form until around the late twelfth century, they still contained truthful, historical notes about the times and events spoken of. The Hemings Pattr is an example of a tale in the old tradition. It is about a fictional hero, but the hero is placed into an actual historical event. It was written to both entertain and inform.

Here is a section from the saga. It is worth noting the similarities with other accounts of the aftermath of the Battle at Hastings.

Hemings Pattr

William the Bastard was ruling over Normandy, as has been mentioned before. He hears about King Haraald's invasion of England. He sends messengers all over his kingdom and summons to himself a great army. Then he addresses them and says:

> 'You are aware what became of the fellowship between
> me and Harold Godwinnson. Now I hear that an army is
> invading his kingdom. I now intend to go with this army
> here to avenge him if anything has happened to him.

Moreover, there will never be another time when it will be easier to take vengeance on Harold for the dishonour he has done me, and to stake my claim to England, even if he has been victorious, for all his bravest men will be wounded and battle-weary.'

> Now on the day that William rode out of Rúðuborg,
> then his queen went up to him just as he had mounted
> his horse and took hold of his stirrup, wanting to speak
> to him. But he drives his spurs into the horse and she falls
> in front of the horse and the horse tramples over her and
> she was killed instantly.
> He spoke: 'Evil happenings are portents of good to
> follow. It is very likely that our expedition will turn out
> well.'
> After that they board ship and sail to England, and he
> starts to ravage the land as soon as he enters the country.
> It is said that he had Ívarr the Boneless cremated before
> he began to plunder.

> King Harold hears about this and summons his men
> together. His people were just now in the worst condition.

The king tells them to clear out of the country if they thought themselves unable to support him, but they all said they wanted to support him.

The king says: 'You will be handing me over [to our enemies] if you don't support me loyally.' They said they would never desert him. He advances with his army against William and a fierce battle takes place there. This was nineteen nights after King Harald Sigurðarson fell.

There are many casualties there among the Englishmen, for there were many took part in the battle that were not fit for anything. They fight the whole day, and in the evening King Harold Godwinsson fell. But they, Hemingr and Helgi and Valþjófr, get into a wedge-shaped formation and here their opponents are making no headway.

Then William spoke: 'I will spare you, Valþjófr, if you will swear me an oath of loyalty. Then you may keep your inheritance and your Earldom.'

Valþjófr says: 'I won't swear you any oaths. But I will promise to be true to you, if you will do as you say.' 'We shall make peace on these terms,' said Viljálmr. Valþjófr asked: 'What terms shall Hemingr and Helgi have, if they make peace?'

William answers:

'Helgi shall keep his inheritance and Earldom. He shall swear loyalty to me, and advise me on all matters about which he can see more clearly than I. And Hemingr shall stay with me, and if he is true to me, then I shall honour him most highly.'

Valþjófr asks: 'What do you both want to do?' Helgi answers: 'Let Hemingr decide.'

Hemingr answers: 'I know that you Englishmen must think it about time to bring an end to all this warfare, but I shall take no pleasure in life after this battle. But nevertheless I will not force you to risk your lives any longer than you wish. But it is my opinion that the truce will be short-lived for Valþjófr.'

Valþjófr answers: 'It is better for us to be overthrown than to refuse to trust anyone, and no more men shall die on my account.' They give up the battle and accept a truce.

Then William was made king and they rode thence to London. Valþjófr asked leave to go home and received it, and rode away in a party of twelve. The king glanced after them and said: 'It is inadvisable to let a man ride off scot-free who refuses to swear us oaths, so ride after him and kill him.' And they did so. Valþjófr dismounted and forbade his companions to defend him. He went to a church and was killed there and there he is buried. And people think of him as a saint. King Harold Godwinsson healed The night after King Harold Godwinsson had fallen, then a certain peasant and his wife drove to where the dead lay to strip the dead and get themselves some wealth.

They see there great heaps of dead. They see there a bright light. They discuss this together and say that there must be a saintly man there among the dead.

They now begin to clear away the corpses from where they saw the light. They see a man's arm lift up from among the corpses and there was a large gold ring on it. The peasant took hold of the hand and asked whether the man was alive.

He answers: 'I am alive.' The old woman spoke: 'Clear off the corpses: I think this is the king.' They lifted the man up and ask if it is possible for him to be healed.

The king says: 'I do not deny that I could be healed, but you cannot do it.' The woman spoke: 'We shall have a go.'

They picked him up and put him in their cart and drive home with him.

The woman spoke: 'You must strip the flesh off the carthorse and cut off its ears. And if anyone comes to you looking for the king's corpse, then you must say that I have gone mad, and that wolves have torn your horse to pieces.'

They cleanse the king's wounds and dress them and keep him with them in secret. A little later King William's men come there and ask why he had taken King Harold home with him, whether he was alive or dead.

The old man answers: 'I have not done that.'

They answered: 'It's no use denying it, for there is the trail of blood leading to your premises.' The man says: 'I am not at all concerned about the loss of your king. I am more concerned about the loss of my carthorse, that wolves tore to pieces the other night when the battle had taken place.'

They answered: 'That is no doubt true, for we saw the horse here torn to pieces. But even so we intend to go in here and find out what is going on.' The man spoke: 'Misfortunes never cease to come upon me. My wife went mad from hearing the trumpets and battle-cries.'

They insist on going in all the same. And when they get inside, there was the old woman sitting by the fire eating coal. And when she sees the men, she jumps up and grabs a carving knife and swears and threatens to kill them.

They go out laughing at her and go home without more ado, and tell the king they cannot find King Harold's corpse. But the old woman and her husband heal the king in secret until he was better.

Then the king sends the old woman to Hemingr and she tells him where the king was. Hemingr says: 'I hope, grandma, that you know what you are saying now.'

The old woman answers: 'I was not mad.'

The next day Hemingr comes to the king and there took place there a very joyful reunion. They talk together the whole of that day. Hemingr offers the king to go all over the country collecting an army together. 'And you could soon get the kingdom back from William'

The king spoke: 'I realise that this may be possible, but then too many will become perjurers. And I don't want so much evil to happen on my account. Now I am going to follow the example of King Óláfr Tryggvason, who, after he was defeated off Vinðland, decided then not to return to his kingdom, but instead went out to Greece and there served God as long as he lived. Now I am going to have a hermit's cell made for me in Canterbury, where I shall be able see King William as often as possible in the church. And the only food I shall have is what you bring me.' Hemingr agrees to this.

The king gives the old man and his wife a suitable reward, and afterwards goes into a hermitage. He stays there for three years without anyone knowing who he is except Hemingr and the priest that confessed him. And one day when Hemingr came to see Harold, then he tells him that he has caught a sickness that will bring about his death. And one day, when King William was sitting at table, bells were heard ringing all over the town. The king asks why such a fine peal is being rung.

Hemingr answers: 'I guess that a certain monk, who was called Harold, has died.' 'What Harold is he?' says the king.

'Godwinsson,' says Hemingr. 'Who has kept him hidden?' says the king. Hemingr answers: 'I have done it.'

'If this is true,' says the king, 'then you shall die for it. But we shall look at his corpse.' After that he goes into the cell where the body lay. It was then stripped. Everyone then recognised King Harold. The corpse was beautiful and pleasant to look at, and people smelt there a sweet smell, so that everyone present there realised that he was a truly saintly man.

Then the king asked Hemingr what he would undertake to do to earn a reprieve.

Hemingr asked: 'What do you require me to do, king?'

'I want you to swear me this, that you will be as loyal to me in every way as you have been to King Harold, and to serve me as you have done him.' Hemingr says: 'I would rather die with him than live with you. But I could have betrayed you long ago if I had wanted to.'

'It is very true,' said the king, 'that England will be the poorer by one of the bravest men if you are killed. Now I will offer to make you the noblest baron in England, and to make you a member of my personal following, and put you in sole charge of it; alternatively, if you do not want this, I will give you an annuity of three hundred pounds every twelve months, and you may live wherever you like in England.' Hemingr thanked the king for his offers and spoke:

'I will accept your offer to let me stay in England, but I have no desire to possess wealth from now on. But this request I make of you, that you will give me permission and let me have this same cell, and in it I will end my days.'

The king was silent for a long time, and then spoke: 'Because this request is made with purity of intention, it shall be granted you.'

Afterwards William had the body of King Harold clothed in royal robes and gave him a most fitting funeral. And he was buried with the greatest honour. Soon after Hemingr entered the afore-mentioned cell and there served God until his old age, and finally became blind, and he died in that hermitage.

After reading through this saga, it seems possible that there was a sharing of stories, of accounts, and it is worth noting that where these stories all draw similarities is around the finding of Harold and his being carried away. These events are the same: found, near death, under a pile of corpses, a woman asking if he is alive, him exclaiming that he is alive. Yes, these are stories to entertain, it's true, yet always with a strong, factual, and historical thread.

The nameless writer of the Vita Haroldi explains how those with him who were witness to these events were bound by a moral code, as would befit godly folk, to tell the truth even though most of the chroniclers had not.

In summary, although the evidence from these sources is read as hearsay, the places, circumstances, and events of those times harmonise. Critics have argued that Harold was a king, a proud man who would have fought to the death to save his kingdom, adding that he was not that kind of character who could change so easily.

Yet history tells us of kings and nobles of those times who had turned to penitence, rejecting their former lives and living austere lives.

It is what we say about slanderous accusations: 'words are cheap'. As the anonymous historian said at the beginning, historians will write of events, however 'the truth is wrecked'.

～

In conclusion, after having looked into his life before and after the battle, I have to say that Harold was a well-educated and charismatic man of striking good looks. He was a principled man and a good king.

The false stories? I believe these stories were propaganda—the stories that he swore on a heap of holy relics to give William the throne.

I believe he was loved by his people and highly respected by all who met him. He was a powerful soldier over six feet one inches, able, it is said, to slaughter both knight and horse in one stroke of his sword. If it is a myth, it was coordinated between religious houses in secret and in separate lifetimes. Such facts as these must strengthen the feasibility of this study we have undertaken.

So, where is our smoking gun?

1. The testimonies
2. The Saracen nurse

How many coincidences must we pass over before we decide that these are strong arguments, and so we must consider the hermit tale as the more probable story so that these findings are then given serious consideration? We have the testimonies of the church, the records written by scribes whose sole purpose was to record for future generations the true histories of the English church and its people. We have the testimonies of those ancient historians, men without an agenda who wrote from the testimonies of local people. We have Gurth's testimony, recorded for us by the church fathers, as well as his description of Herbaltown, 'the rock', 'the cave', 'the cleansing sacrifices', and the herbalist whose knowledge of medicine was so well-known and respected that healers from the farthest reaches of these isles journeyed to her for these cures and obscure plants.

The Saracen Nurse

I am convinced that we have found the Saracen nurse, who was called upon by those close to the king in their king's darkest hour to heal Harold. Subsequently, the close bond that this extended period of time together formed between them both resulted in the birth of their daughter. This young black girl, until now identified as the angel Gabriel, holding an African feather fan with a friendly smile, had red hair inherited from her father. This, we believe, is the daughter of King Harold II, pictured opposite her mother in the north window of that small stone building that had been for centuries the leper hospital of St Nicholas, Harbledown.

Is Harold the hermit buried at his church at Waltham? Is it a myth that he survived the battle and lived to a ripe old age as a penitent? We will know, if we are allowed to exhume the unmarked grave at the east wall of Waltham. I am convinced, and yes, I believe he lived to a good age indeed; it would mean that he outlived all his enemies, and he lived not only to see a Saxon queen on the throne of England but also to hear of the successful invasion of Normandy by an English king on 14 October 1106, forty years after the Battle of Hastings to the day.

There are other ponderables that have an association with Harold, and one I particularly like is a tale spoken of another hermit of Chester. This requires—no, demands—more of my time, limited though it is, for I am of an age that prohibits optimism when faced with as lengthy an investigation as has been in this Harold endeavour.

Henry IV, Emperor of Alemanni

Should I venture down this path? I wonder, though it is intriguing and has a strong connection to this tale of Harold's. It was in those days just prior to Harold becoming king that a young Henry IV became ruler in Germany. His father had died in 1053, and at the age of three Henry was crowned. At the age of fifteen, he had befriended Harold, the earl and next king of England. The actual details of how this came about are a matter for further research, and for the moment I can only reason on this by looking at how those interstate relationships worked back then.

Harold was a frequent traveller as a senior statesman at the time, and in Alemannia (Germany) he had relatives and, therefore, close ties for him personally. From the wording in the Vita Haroldi, in the section that talks about the king or emperor of Alemanni, it discusses the concern the king had on hearing that 'his friend', Harold, Earl of Wessex, had a mysterious form of paralysis. The obvious age difference between Harold and Henry was not questioned or even mentioned in the manuscript, however for the record, I would estimate that it was significant, around twenty-eight years. So what form did this friendship take?

I noted from the text in the Vita Haroldi that it is the young king who, on hearing of the illness, sent his physician, Ailard, to assist. By today's standards, this may seem a little odd, yet back in medieval times, a young king wielded power, albeit controlled to some extent by those advisors behind the throne, in this case his mother, Agnes of Poitou. This period is interesting. From Henry's investiture until his being kidnapped by Archbishop Anno II at the age of eleven, this was the period I would guess when a connection between the very young Henry and Harold was made.

His mother, Agnes, sought alliances with people of power in order to secure Henry's place. I would hazard an educated guess that she sought the support of Harold too. As a powerful earl and with family connections to Germany and Saxony, Harold could have been of considerable advantage to the young king. The writer of the Vita Haroldi was copying from earlier notes, as we know, and looking back in retrospect. Therefore despite the fact that the young Henry would not have as yet ascended to the throne as emperor until 1084, Henry would have been known to the writer as the king and emperor.

Looking at the dates, we have an acknowledgement that Harold was considered a friend of the king of Alemanni and that in 1065, Henry IV, after taking up his role as king and administrator of Alemannia, sent his own personal physician to assist Harold.

Now, jumping forward in time with Harold, we are in the year 1105. While in Cheswardine, Shropshire, Harold had word that the Anchorite cell at St James, Chester, had become vacant, because its former occupant, Henry IV, referred to by the historian Gerald of Wales as 'Emperor of Rome', had died. We know this date was 1105 because it was stated in the Latin text of the meeting between Gurth and King Henry I at Woodstock that Harold died in this same cell in 1112.

If we do the math, Harold was living in that Anchorite cell for seven years, and that means it was 1105 when the death of the hermit, known locally as Henry IV, former emperor of Alemannia, occurred. History tells us that Henry IV was born in 1050 and died in 1105.

We know that Henry IV relinquished the throne to his son Henry V, but there is some confusion as to dates around this time. It is said by some authorities that he died without absolution from his excommunication, yet his very location at the time of his death tells me it is likely that this was not so. I presume to suggest that the brothers at St John's, Chester, would have been on hand to ease his passing as a comfort to him.

It is known that after his son took his title, Henry IV sought advice from a Lotharingian noble, and although the location of the province of Lotharingia was on the coastline of what is now northern France and Belgium, there was a Lotharingian noble named Robert, who was the bishop of Hereford. This is interesting because it now adds credibility as to how, if the history of Chester has truthfulness at its core, Henry could have ended his days at Chester. Again we have to look at the proposed dates offered by the various historical records of the time, and these vary. We also need to look seriously at recorded whereabouts of all these players in this fascinating investigation.

The times of these characters' various dates of births and deaths, followed by the recorded sequence of events whatever the actual time lines dictate, are important. Henry IV was considered a close friend of Harold as a young king, and the sequence of events, as we have just looked at, fits within the time frames that easily place Harold and Henry IV together at those most critical times.

Was Harold one of Henry's close mentors and amongst his dearest of friends, as is stated in the Vita Haroldi? Was Harold aware that this old friend and the former emperor of Germany was in the small cell in Chester? I like to think so, and I like to think that they were united at some time. After all, Harold was in the vicinity for a number of years before actually moving into the hermit's cell.

But what of those days when Harold sought assistance from the Saxon and German nobles, from 1068 to 1072? Would he have harboured some resentment for being turned down by the young Henry?

After looking at the situation in those days, it would have become clear to Harold that revolt was close with the Saxony uprising around that time. It would be logical to conclude that Harold would realise that Henry had his own problems, and a speculative and costly campaign into a Norman-held England would not be sensible.

I have nothing other than disputed documents and circumstantial evidence in relation to this Henry IV and Harold connection, however it follows a logic that cannot quickly be dismissed, for who can deny the right for me to assemble all known information? Should I not offer up this scenario and conclude that those events in the lives of those two men are as I have laid out?

Unmarked Grave at the East Wall of the Church in Waltham Abbey

If we ever get permission to uncover the remains of King Harold, we will know how close this book is to the truth of the life and death of our last Saxon king, Harold II. They are just 45 centimetres below the lawned surface. Eighteen inches in English.

So close, yet so far.

The Last Confession of William I

I've persecuted the natives of England beyond all reason, whether gentle or simple. I have cruelly oppressed them and unjustly disinherited them, killed innumerable multitudes by famine or the sword and become the barbarous murderer of many thousands both young and old of that fine race of people, having gained the throne of that kingdom by so many crimes I dare not leave it to anyone but God to judge.

—Orderic Vitalis

This 'last confession' William recorded is very revealing.

I remember my grandfather, Harry Eade, who fought in the Great War—the war to end all wars, as those poor chaps were told. I remember this sweeping statement he once made: 'There were not many atheists in the trenches.' He was not the only old soldier to make this comment. This was a period of time when many homes had a Bible, unless they were Catholic homes, because the local priest saw it as his duty to let his flock know what was written in the good book. Nevertheless, it was a part of the way of life back then, prior to the First World War, that families had a family Bible. The children went to Sunday school, we had hymns sung in schools all over Europe, and the church was a great influence in the communities back then. People had a faith, and this was especially evident when ordinary people faced those last moments on this earth, when they turned their attention to that place all must face, that dark chasm that draws you in and tests all those doubts and fears, and a faith that may not be up to the task of calming that fear of what is to become of you when you cross over from life to death.

Who was at William's side at that most daunting and fearful time?

Would he have drawn comfort from the words of the cardinal, his family, or his friends? His words show that he could not dare to trust the conciliatory platitudes of any who would wish to ease his journey onward, having the belief that only God can see into the heart of a man.

This one thought at such a time would wither the stout heart of the most fearless of men. And so I wonder, What memory from William's long, warring past would he have given consideration to at that extreme moment of clarity?

'Having gained the throne of that kingdom by so many crimes, I dare not leave to any but God to judge.'

Honest words indeed. It brings into focus his true feelings about the church at the time. It would be a sobering lesson for any who had faith in the church, and the holy fathers of the time, even the pope. It was a lesson in whom to trust when the chips were down! This former faith he had had in men, this pope, and the representation of Christ on earth? William would sweep these and their placatory words of comfort to the side, knowing the corruption and lies they had joined in with him, remembering the papal banner, the blessing of his campaign, and the lies about Harold.

At this most poignant of times, I have no doubt these last words of William were a stab to the heart of those of the cloth who were witness to this confession. His only hope of redemption, in his eyes at that moment, was to trust only in his creator. He dared do nothing else.

This was a sobering reminder to me, when in life you justify actions by listening to the words of men, whether of the cloth or not. We can search our own hearts and judge for ourselves not what we can and can't do but what we should or shouldn't do.

William was no different, and looking back on the lives of both Harold and William, in 1066 it was William who lowered the dragon banner, golden and proud. Yet in the final sum of both men's lives, it was Harold who fared the better, for he shed the mantle of the fighting man, turned away from a life carved out for him from an early age, and sought no longer a life of fame and glory but a road on which he would find peace. He accepted a life as a penitent, and in so doing, he slew the dragon.

I see the road Harold chose as a good choice, a noble choice, and it was a road that, in his mind, could lead to redemption. That road would give him peace, and so it was a road that was the more profitable for him.

We have looked at this curious tale told to us by those monks at Waltham. Together we have looked at the evidence. What conclusion do we arrive at? I believe that the evidence points to Harold surviving and living the better life, being cared for as a simple pilgrim by the church that, it is said, excommunicated him but then fed him and at times clothed and housed him.

I believe in the latter part of his life, he lived more peacefully and probably more honestly than the earlier part. He proved that peace comes from within and has nothing to do with power, possessions, or privilege—a lesson learned too late for his adversary, William.

After having looked at the case for Harold the hermit, you must decide which to believe.

Slaying the Dragon
The East Wall at Waltham Abbey

The pale square is where we located the unmarked grave

REFERENCES

1. Vita Haroldi Harlien, MS 3776.
2. Thomas de Burton and Edward Augustus Bond, *Chronica Monasterii de Melsa: A fundatione usque ad annum 1396*, vol. 1, p. 153 [Google Books].
3. Higdens Polychronicon-Ranulphi Castrensis Cognomine Higden, Polychronicon [sive-historia Polycratica] ab inito mundi usque ad mortem regis Edward III in septem libros dispositum. 1326.
4. http://codexceltica.blogspot.co.uk/2007/08/man-in-a-cloth-mask.html.
5. http://www.chesterwalls.info/stjohn.html.
6. Gerald of Wales.
7. Master Wace continuator, ref. to Harold: 'He that wishes to know this, at Waltham, behind the high altar, can find this self-same altar an Harold lying in the choir.' In P. J. Huggins, 'The Church at Waltham: An Archaeological and Historical Review'.
8. Harbledoun St Nicholas Church, Leper Hospital. Location of the 'Rock' noted in the days of Lanfranc as the place for herbal healing.
9. Magnus Barelegs at the Battle of Ulster (*Uladstir*).

INSIDE LEAF ACKOWLEDGEMENTS. My thanks to the editorial team for their dedication and patience, to Clive Simpson, Annie Sabbagh, for their support. My Family, and of course, Frances my wife, without her dedication, skills and intuition I would have lacked the energy needed to discover the truth about Harold, and solve the mysteries that have for years surrounded this fascinating tale.

Lightning Source UK Ltd.
Milton Keynes UK
UKHW010627261121
394640UK00001B/93